*Flying-Fox in a Freedom Tree*

# *Flying-Fox*
## *in a*
### *Freedom Tree*

**AND OTHER STORIES**

**Albert Wendt**

University of Hawai'i Press
Honolulu

First published by Longman Paul Limited, 1974

©1974 Albert Wendt

©1999 University of Hawai'i Press
Printed in the United States of America
04  03  02  01  00  99    5  4  3  2  1

**Library of Congress Cataloging-in-Publication Data**
Wendt, Albert, 1939–
   Flying-fox in a freedom tree and other stories / Albert Wendt.
     p.   cm.
   ISBN 0–8248–1823–7 (alk. paper)
   1. Islands of the Pacific—Social life and customs—Fiction.
2. Western Samoa—Social life and customs—Fiction.   I. Title.
PR9665.9.W46F59   1999
823—dc21                         99–32575
                                          CIP

"A Descendant of the Mountain" has appeared previously in *Landfall,* and
"Virgin-wise" in *Argot.*

University of Hawai'i Press books are printed on acid-free
paper and meet the guidelines for permanence and
durability of the Council on Library Resources.

Printed by Cushing-Malloy

*In memory of my grandmother Mele Tuaopepe, the greatest
storyteller I have ever known*

# Contents

# A Descendant of the Mountain

The influenza epidemic squatted over the district of Fale-
fanua that lay spread-eagled beneath the impersonal
mountain, hatching her brood of death. The epidemic had
crawled over the mountain range from the western side of
the island after flying across the Pacific in a sailing ship and
lodged in the throats of white sailors who spewed it out on
reaching the shore. Now it was free under a sun that hung
from the copper sky like a judge, a sun that cast a harsh
spell of light over the mountain range, the village, the trees,
the beach, and the sea.

In the fale, sitting crosslegged like a statue, Mauga – high
chief of the district – drank the wailing and chanting of the
mourners as he stared at the body of his wife stretched out
in the middle of the pebble floor and covered with fine mats.
Flies swirled round the face of the dead woman. Mauga
broke from the spell with the shrill sound of the song of a
bird. Then the pain was there again, snaking its way from
the core of his belly to fill his mouth and brim over from
his eyes. He looked out. A troupe of mourners – now a daily
sight – trailed past on the road. They bore a long bundle
and headed surely for the graveyard. Soon they too would
have to follow that road with the body of his wife. Mauga
shuddered. First his eldest son – heir to his name – had died ;
then one of his daughters ; now it was his wife. A fuia
streaked past the fale, and Mauga caught it in the corner of
his eyes till the bird disappeared into the shelter of the trees.
Mauga blinked, controlled the twitching of his body, and
commanded : 'Enough of this !' The wailing ceased immediately. 'She is dead. That is all. She is dead and gone to

God!' He paused, compelled to stop and choke the swelling tongue of pain that had reached his clenched teeth, threatening to give the lie to all his outward show of strength. 'It is God's will,' he whispered. For a moment, in the stifling heat, he grew cold like a knife blade, and he stood up and hurried out of the fale, stopping the funeral while everyone watched him disappear over the road into the trees.

Hidden by the banana trees, he sat down muttering: 'It's God's will. . . . It's God's will,' as if he was attempting to persuade himself that it was so. He had lost count of the days since the epidemic started, and of the number of victims it had claimed. Only the pain and fear of the inexplicable terror was real. He stretched out under the trees and deliberately opened his eyes to absorb the hurt of the blaring light. In his head there were no clear pictures, just an infuriating dark without any trace of the seeds of understanding. Like muscle round the bone, the dark had claimed him as it had claimed the rest of his people. A spider, dangling from a banana leaf above him, edged down toward his eyes. He watched it steadily; then his hand shot up, closed round it, killed it. Some understanding flicked into his mind as he examined the dead spider on the palm of his hand. Yes, God had willed the epidemic to punish him and his people. His eyes shut tightly as he listened to the faraway tolling of the church lali. Another victim. God was angry, and His anger knew no bounds. This was the explanation which Mauga shared with his people. Mauga turned over and staggered to his feet. The funeral wailing seeped through the trees again at that moment and iced him to the ground. The sound came whistling like sea-wind chopping the fingers of the trees. Wailing as terrifying as spears probing the moulded clay of his skull. Caught in the sound of the chant and wooden drum, like the harmony of bone round the marrow, Mauga throbbed with fear as the wailing battled to snuff out the flicker of light in his mind. Chained, he watched the leaves dance down to the quivering roots with the heat like wax round his body. As the tolling of the lali and the wailing ebbed away like a setting sun, Mauga shook his body as if to expel the dark from himself into the air and the trees. He gazed up, up at the sun crucified to the centre of the sky. *There was no longer anywhere to hide*. He turned and stumbled deeper and deeper into the web of trees.

He stopped suddenly. The clearing – a green carpet of creepers and fern – skimmed away from his feet and broke abruptly to his right, where a spring bubbled like coconut milk from the earth to form a round, deep pool. He dragged his body to the pool, pushing forward, and watched his mouth sucking greedily at the water. He sighed and belched as the water stunned his belly. It was good. For a long while he lay, contemplating his reflection in the water. Gradually he forgot the terrifying reality of the epidemic as memories of his youth bubbled up from the mudbank of his mind, memories as captivating and pure as the water under his face. Seeds of memory burst and filled his head and heart, driving out the bitter dark. He sat up. He pulled his lavalava above his knees and dangled his legs into the water. Slowly the coolness of the water tingled up from his legs and revived his whole body. A breeze tinkled through the trees and caressed his greying hair. A picture focused in Mauga's head. He had seen her stepping from the trees: the girl Fanua who was to become his wife. Tall and slender she had emerged out of the womb of trees. He had remained, as he was now, staring into the water, pretending he had not seen her. She filled his eyes like soothing ointment as she stopped, startled by the sight of the young man sitting by the pool, her pool.

As she walked cautiously toward him, he continued to watch her out of the corner of his eye. She shuddered and folded her arms protectively over her naked breasts. Without looking at him, she circled the pool and sat down on the other side. Casually she scooped up handfuls of water and drank them as though saying: 'This pool is mine!' His head came up, and he caught her staring almost angrily at him.

'I only came to have a drink,' he heard himself apologise. She said nothing. And, as if he wasn't there, she drew her lavalava high above her knees, exposing her soft thighs to the sunlight and to his eyes as she stuck her legs into the water. He looked away politely. She didn't seem to care. She placed her arms behind her to support her weight and,

3

as she yawned and stretched her body, her breasts tautly challenged him. From narrowed eyes he drank the whole of her beauty, suddenly becoming conscious of his heart thudding against his ribs. He looked away, ashamed, feeling annoyed, for somehow he believed that her actions were deliberate attempts to drive him away from the pool. He wasn't going to leave!

'Who do you think you are?' he called to her. She stared straight back at him. Immediately he felt a fool. He sprang up and moved to leave. She laughed. He paused.

'Don't go!' she called. 'I'll leave if you want me to.'

He turned to face her, sensing that there was some trace of understanding between them: she was willing to share the pool with him. She smiled at him. And he noticed that she had pulled down her lavalava, and that her arms were again crossed over her breasts. He sighed in relief, but he was disappointed that she no longer looked natural, free. The sun was now over the trees, and the sunlight filtered through the leaves and branches to lie calmly on the surface of the water. The heat was lifting. The throbbing chorus of the cicadas pulsated in their ears in unison with the beating of their hearts.

'I'm going to bathe. It'll be dark soon,' she called. She pulled off her lavalava. He blushed and turned his back even though he wanted so much to look at her. When he heard the splash as her body cut into the water, he turned round slowly.

'It's good,' she remarked, her body swallowed up to the neck by the water. Her hair, now wet and pinned to her head and neck by the weight of the dive, glistened like black lava. 'Why don't you come in?' she invited him.

He started. He could almost hear her giggling. She twisted and dived for the bottom of the pool. When she was completely out of sight, he whipped off his lavalava and dived in. Once under, in the cool green water, he opened his eyes. She hovered straight in front of him, and, while her head was out of the water, the golden nakedness of the rest of her body confronted him full in the face and injected desire into his bones. He stopped, and hurried to the surface to find her laughing as she blinded him with water. Their

4

laughter mated and lost itself in the dense trees and the fading light.

Three weeks later he took her for his wife as naturally as she had shown herself to him at the pool.

A crackling in the trees broke the spell. . . . *Now she was dead.* . . . Mauga sat up immediately. The delicate picture was gone, shattered by the footsteps cracking over the brittle undergrowth toward him. He dashed his puffed face with water and awaited the intruder.

It was his son Timu who came into view with his head bowed. His feet marked a thin trail over the creepers till he stood above his father, staring down. The boy, aged about eleven, placed his hand lightly on his father's head. Mauga turned slowly under the boy's hand till his eyes found his son's grinning face, then his arms circled the boy's waist and drew him to him. This was his last son, the remaining heir to his title: Mauga. Mauga the Mountain, centuries old, as old as the history of the village, an institution now threatened with destruction by the wrath of God who seemed so far away – burning like an indifferent star outside his vision – yet so immediately terrifying. Bitterness and protest festered in Mauga's heart as the picture of his dead wife erupted into his mind.

'God! God! God!'

The boy heard his father's pitiful voice cut into his side. He had never seen his father like this before, helpless and human like most men. To him, his father had always been the Rock, the Mountain, unapproachable and high like the mountain behind the village, the mountain from which his family was descended. The boy gazed down at his father for a long time, as though the next thing he might do was to censure his father for behaving like a child and not in keeping with his high rank. When he became chief he would never act like this. Hadn't his father told him this?

When he moved it was an attempt to leave, but his father's arm held him, as securely as the history and mana of the title chained his father. So the boy stood, slowly melting under the fire of love which he felt for his father, till he was as pure as the water beside him, and he wrapped his arms like comforting shields round his father's head. The man was no longer the mountain, impersonal and far away. The man was truly his father who now needed his love – as much as he had needed the love which his father had never given him.

Mauga straightened suddenly and pushed his son away. Enough of that. He was Mauga. He bowed his head with his face turned away from the boy's eyes, ashamed for having shown so vulnerably that he was like other men.

'The funeral is over,' the boy informed the man. 'Mother's funeral is over.' Mauga's face showed no emotion. This annoyed the boy, gradually turned his love to anger. Stepping forward he picked up a large rock with both hands, and hurled it into the pool. He turned then and ran across the clearing and disappeared into the trees.

Mauga hugged himself as the rock shattered his reflection and pushed waves to the banks, as the mud rose steadily from the bottom of the pool like dark sleep. Soon the pool was quivering mud. Mauga jumped to his feet and fled toward the trees, stumbling for home and the tolling lali. Over his shoulder he glanced back at the mountain range. centring his eyes on the highest peak. Mauga stood crowned by the last rays of the setting sun.

# The Cross of Soot

Behind him the hibiscus hedge was bursting crimson boils of flowers; the morning breeze played with the lizard tongues of the sugar-cane trees rooted into the mud bank of the stream; a twisted breadfruit tree threw a fungus of shadows over the boy busy clearing the grass with short pecking movements of his hands; and, above all the greenness and the many sounds of the morning world, the sun sailed – a copper emblem stitched on to a flag of crystal blue.

The boy picked up an empty bucket and ran to the stream. Crabs flicked back into their dark holes. He knelt and scooped handfuls of pasty mud and flung them thudding into the bucket till it was full, then, wiping his hands clean with the end of his lavalava, he sprang up, picked up the bucket and staggered back to the shadow of the breadfruit tree, where he tipped the mud on to the ground, sat down before it and began moulding his great fortress.

A segasegamou shot impatiently across the sky, dived down towards the stream and disappeared into the sugar-cane. The image of the fortress was clear in his mind, but his hands could not release it into the mud which oozed through his fingers, refusing to be tamed into shape. Taking a bushknife he tried carving the pulpy mass but again he failed. Swearing under his breath he stood up and sent the whole mound of mud flying with one swift kick. He turned and skipped towards the bank of the stream, stopped and scanned the other side.

The prison compound was fenced in by a high barbed-wire fence. The jail – a large square concrete building – stood white and bleached. The boy picked up a stone and skimmed it across the water. He heard it clatter against the side of the building. A steel pipe extended across the stream. He giggled as he walked over the pipe, pulling faces at his reflection in the water.

He snaked himself under the barbed-wire fence, stood up, brushed the dirt from his hands and knees, stooped down and began wading through the green lake of taro leaves, toward the jail. He was wet with dew by the time he reached the building. He laughed softly as he hugged the side of the building. It was a great game.

He peered round the corner of the jail. Smoke was billowing from the roof of the small fale after rising angrily from a sparking umu bedded in the middle of the earthen floor. Behind it, in the middle of the compound, an old man sat before a valusaga scraping breadfruit and singing, the fat of his arms wobbling in time to the scraping, his grey hair shimmering in the light. The boy moved stealthily away from the jail and tiptoed towards the old man, holding his hand over his mouth, stopping himself from laughing.

He tapped the old man's head and jumped back, laughing. The old man turned abruptly.

'Oh, it's you!' he sighed. 'You gave me a fright!'

The boy grinned and sat down cross-legged beside him.

'You should be at school,' said the old man.

'Our headmaster died,' said the boy. 'A ghost entered him and killed him.'

The old man guffawed and said, 'Didn't you like him?'

The boy shook his head: he didn't like many of his other teachers either. He didn't understand why the old man was laughing: he truly believed that a ghost had killed the headmaster.

'Did you ever go to school?' he asked the old man. The old man looked away. The boy repeated his question.

'No,' said the old man. 'Never had the chance. . . . Who wants to go to school, anyway?'

'I don't, but my father wants me to,' said the boy, picking at his nose.

The old man tossed him a scraper. 'Help me scrape the breadfruit. Use the valusaga over there.'

The boy took the scraper and went and sat down at the

other valusaga. The old man rolled some breadfruit over to him. The boy picked one up and started scraping it.

They worked in silence as the sun rose slowly toward noon and chased the shadows to the bases of the trees and buildings. Flies buzzed around the boy and the old man, biting at the open sores on the boy's legs. He didn't feel them, he was used to flies. The stench of the stream grew stronger as the mud dried.

'Sure wish they didn't put lavatories on the stream,' the old man said for lack of anything else to say. (He was used to the smell.)

'Very smelly, isn't it,' said the boy. (He too was used to the stench.) The old man nodded and looked at the boy who was concentrating on scraping the breadfruit. The picture of his own son came into his mind, dark and laughing. He looked away from the boy and worked with more fury on the breadfruit.

'When are you going to leave here?' the boy asked suddenly.

The old man stiffened. He reached up and wiped the sweat off his brow with the end of his lavalava. 'Never,' he said.

'Where were you born?'

'At Lefaga.'

Surprised, the boy stopped working and said, 'But that's where my father is a matai.'

'Yes, that's the place. I knew your father very well when we were boys.' He spoke in a soft monotone, as if by keeping his voice low he would be able to control the pain he was feeling.

Another prisoner, a young man who was thick-lipped, stocky, with flashing eyes and a livid bushknife scar on his left cheek, stumbled into the compound, carrying a carton of tinned herrings.

The boy looked up and greeted him. 'Have you come?'

'Look what we got,' the young prisoner said to the old man, ignoring the boy's greeting. 'We're going to have a good feed this week!' The old man dismissed him with a nod. The youth dropped the box to the ground and turned to the boy. 'You know what?' he said to the boy, but looking steadily at the old man, 'A new man's coming in today.

I was in Court when the sentence was . . . . You know the case of the Falefa murderer? Well he's been sentenced to . . . . '

The old man stopped him from finishing. 'Put the box over there and go get some bananas.' It was a command. The youth looked at the old man, the scar on his cheek seemed to glow. The boy looked at him, then at the old man. The youth snapped his eyes away from the old man, finally. The boy relaxed: the old man had won.

As the youth walked away, the boy picked up the scraper and continued working.

'How is your grandmother?' the old man asked him after a while.

'She's well, thank you,' the boy replied, noticing with interest that the old man had five black warts on the back of his right hand.

'That's good,' said the old man. 'My mother was like . . . . ' He stopped.

'How long have you been here?' asked the boy just for the sake of talking.

The old man paused for a moment, thinking about it, and then said, 'Five years.' He looked at the ground.

'Why?' asked the boy, wishing now that he hadn't taken on the job of scraping. His hands were aching and covered with the sticky sap of the breadfruit.

The old man stopped working. 'Would you like to go and get us a pail of water?' he asked the boy, deliberately changing the subject. The boy sprang up and ran towards the tap round the corner of the jail. The scraper dropped as the old man's hand rose up and closed tightly over his face.

He straightened when he heard the patter of the boy's feet, picked up the scraper and resumed working. The boy placed the bucket beside the old man and sat down facing him. When the old man didn't say anything the boy watched the trails of sweat on the old man's shoulders, magnifying them into huge rivers storming down to the sea, drowning everything in their way.

He grew bored with rivers and asked the old man why the youth who had brought the carton of herrings had been put in prison.

'Oh, he raped a girl,' said the old man.

'Uh?' replied the boy. Not knowing what rape meant but pretending that he knew, he added, 'How long is he going to be here?' Knowing that the boy didn't understand what rape was, the old man chuckled. The boy told him that he didn't like the youth.

A kapok cloud crossed the sun and the youth came back carrying a basket of bananas: he was frowning.

'Peel them!' the old man ordered as the youth threw the basket down to the ground. The youth stood clenching and unclenching his fists. 'Peel them!' repeated the old man. The boy stiffened as he saw the youth's eyes shift to a bush-knife which lay like a frozen snake beside the old man's feet.

'Don't!' warned the old man as the youth moved towards the bushknife. The youth hesitated. The boy stooped forward, picked up the bushknife and laid it across his knees. He looked at the youth who turned, sat down hard, picked up a banana and began peeling it. The boy sat caressing the cold blade of the bushknife. He stared at the youth who sat hunched up tight like a clenched fist.

The boy remained still, feeling warm as he nursed his moment of triumph. He had stopped something terrible from happening – even though he didn't quite know what it might have been. He looked up at the sky. The cloud no longer blocked the sun. The lonely pandanus trees on the banks of the stream seemed to stretch their long sword leaves towards him. He shuddered, stuck the bushknife into the earth and moved away from it. He sat down next to the old man, as if he was escaping from some quivering violence to the warmth of something good and wholesome.

Someone tapped him on the shoulder. He looked up. A dark mountain of a laughing young man loomed high above him. The young man, whom they nicknamed 'Samasoni' because they said he was as strong as Samson in the Bible, sat down next to him. The boy punched him playfully.

'How long have you been here?' Samasoni asked.

'Not long,' replied the boy, hugging Samasoni's huge arm and imagining it to be harder than rock.

'What's the matter with our friend over there?' the boy heard Samasoni ask the old man.

11

'Don't know,' replied the old man.

'Samasoni?' interrupted the boy, 'how did you get such big muscles?' The two men laughed. And Samasoni, eyes twinkling with merriment, said, 'I got them by killing a ghost!'

The old man laughed. The boy paused for a while, not knowing whether to believe Samasoni or not. Then he saw the smile on Samasoni's face and he knew and he wished Samasoni would be serious for once.

'Don't worry,' chuckled Samasoni, ruffling the boy's hair. 'You'll have muscles like me some day.' Samasoni held up his right arm and, flexing it, asked the boy to feel it.

'Sure wish I had some like yours!' exclaimed the boy, as he tried strangling Samasoni's bicep. Again the two men laughed.

'Tell him how you crushed that fellow who seduced your sister,' the old man said to Samasoni.

Samasoni shook his head. 'He's too young,' he said.

'No, I'm not,' protested the boy. 'Tell me, please!'

'Alright then. Well, I caught him one night and smashed him up with my fists.' He sprang up like a large cat and demonstrated. His arms flashed like arrows through the air to land with hisses on an invisible opponent. The boy sat with open mouth and watched. He wished he could be proud of his strength as Samasoni was proud of his. Someday he would be, he told himself.

The old man's eyes never left Samasoni as he weaved his power in the air, as his muscles rippled and his face became a symbol of pride. The pain surged up within the old man again, a protest against old age, against the prison life which had gutted him and left him with nothing. He had no future, and he knew that he could no longer do anything to change that. It had to be, but it was difficult to accept an end in nothingness. He staggered up and admitted to himself that he was old, soon to die.

'Finish the breadfruit for me,' he said to Samasoni. There was no power in his voice. Samasoni took his place at the valusaga.

'Can I come with you?' the boy asked the old man.

The old man shook his head. 'The police might see you.' The boy sat down reluctantly.

Samasoni smiled at him. 'Let him go, he is troubled,' he said.

They sat and watched the old man go round the corner of the jail. His feet scraped the bare ground but left little trace that he had passed that way.

The boy glanced at Samasoni and said, 'I sure wish he was my father.'

'Same here,' sighed Samasoni.

The umu in the middle of the fale coughed tongues of fire as the burning logs decayed and crumbled to embers; the stones rolled off it on to the floor.

'Can't you put the stones back on the umu!' Samasoni called to the youth peeling the bananas and who had been watching them all the time. The youth stood up, picked up the iofi and began putting the hot stones back on to the umu. The boy poked his tongue at him. Samasoni winked. The boy giggled.

'Do you know why he was put in here?' Samasoni said to the boy, referring to the youth, and loud enough for him to hear.

Knowing that Samasoni was going to tease the youth, the boy said, 'No!'

'He got here because he beat up a poor helpless chinaman. He nearly killed a poor weak chinaman. The poor man was asleep when that fellow over there attacked him!' Samasoni lied. 'He's not a man.'

'Can I go and help him?' said the boy.

'You'd better,' said Samasoni. 'He's too weak to do anything!'

The boy skipped to the fale, got another pair of iofi and picked up the stones. He tried not to look at the youth. His eyes started crying with the heat of the umu so he turned, gathered up the end of his lavalava and wiped the tears from his eyes.

Suddenly, he felt himself being lifted from the ground, but his hands came up too late to stop himself from hitting the ground, hard. He knew that the youth had pushed him as he felt sharp needles of pain shooting up through his knees and chest. Rolling over to his side he heard Samasoni calling:

'Why did you push him.' It wasn't a question. It was a threat which cleared the sharp ache from the boy's head, as he sprang up to see Samasoni advancing toward the youth.

'I didn't do it deliberately,' muttered the youth, moving away from Samasoni.

'You're a liar,' said Samasoni. 'I saw you!'

'I didn't push him!' insisted the youth.

The boy trembled as he watched Samasoni. He was afraid. He wanted to cry. He closed his eyes and shouted, 'No, Samasoni, he didn't push me. I tripped!' The boy wrapped his arms around his chest. He waited. He hoped. He heard the sound of running feet going away. He opened his eyes. The youth was gone and Samasoni was standing there gazing down at the ground. The boy went to him, took his hand and led him back to the valusaga. Samasoni sat down. The boy sat down beside him.

Disinterestedly, the boy watched a pig spiked like a sea-egg noisily eating pieces of excrement on the edge of the water. He turned and observed Samasoni's hands clutching the breadfruit as though he was trying to squash it into a little ball. And slowly he watched the tenseness ebb out of his friend.

'What's that on your arm?' he asked Samasoni after a while, pointing at a tattoo on Samasoni's left shoulder.

Samasoni relaxed and said, 'An eagle.' He smiled, and the boy felt safe again. 'The old man tattooed it on last week.' Samasoni held up his arm and flexed it, the eagle shimmied up and down as if in flight. The boy laughed.

'Do you think the old man will put one on my arm?' the boy asked.

'Ask him when he comes back.'

'Alright, I'll ask him.' The boy ran his fingers over the place where he hoped the tattoo would go. 'Here he comes now.' He sprang up and ran towards the old man.

But he stopped at a distance when he saw the stranger beside the old man. The stranger was leaning on the old man's shoulder, looking tired and sick. He wore a blue lavalava and a white shirt with a tear on the front. In the

14

man's hand was a tattered Bible. When the two men came up
to him the boy greeted them:

'Have you come?' The stranger started and the boy
noticed that he had been crying. The man straightened up
when he saw the boy. The boy's gaze found grey hairs
sprinkled on the man's head.

'This is Tagi,' the old man introduced the stranger.

The boy nodded his head, sensing that the old man was
feeling awkward standing next to the stranger. 'I hope you
like it here,' the boy said to the man. The man let out a
stifled cry and the boy knew that something was very wrong.
The old man looked at the boy. The boy looked at the
ground, sensing he had done something to hurt the stranger.

'I'm very sorry,' he apologised to the man. He turned and
ran back and sat beside Samasoni.

When the two men came and stood in front of them the
boy noticed that Samasoni was trying his best not to look
at the stranger. The boy wondered why, but he now felt
reluctant asking questions: he didn't want to hurt anyone
anymore.

The old man left the stranger's side and sat down at the
other valusaga which the boy had used. The stranger stood
as if he was rooted to the earth but desiring to grow wings
and fly away from it. There was an awkward silence. The
stranger walked over to the edge of the stream. The boy
started feeling a great liking for him. He wondered why the
man was looking at the water so closely. Perhaps he was
trying to count the pieces of shit as they floated down, he
thought. He had done it often in the past when he had
nothing else to do.

'Nice day isn't it?' Samasoni commented suddenly. His
remark injected into the silence, as huge as his body. The
boy glanced at the stranger, expecting some reply. The
stranger just nodded and kept gazing into the water.

Hesitantly, the boy stood up and, with head bowed,
walked over and sat down by the stranger and dangled his
legs over the edge into the water. The stranger didn't
seem to notice him.

'How many have you counted, Tagi?' the boy asked.

'Uh?' said the stranger.

'I mean how many pieces of shit have you counted?' the boy said. Samasoni and the old man chuckled. The stranger laughed suddenly, the awkwardness gone. And the boy felt that the man was no longer a stranger but one of them.

'Oh, about fifteen,' replied the man. 'I may have miscounted.'

'I don't think so, Tagi. I counted the same.' the boy informed him.

The man sat down beside him. Samasoni threw them a roll of tobacco. Tagi thanked him, pushed open the packet, took out a leaf, and began rolling a cigarette. The boy observed that the man had two of his fingers missing. The wound had only just healed. He wondered why, but knew that it was impolite to ask. The man tried to roll the cigarette: the boy watched him, not offering to help. It was an unwritten law among the prisoners that one should wait till he was asked for help: the boy knew this, and he waited, hoping that Tagi would ask him. The tobacco spilled off the paper and before the man could stoop down and retrieve it the boy reached over and pecked the tobacco off the ground. He took his time handing it back to Tagi.

'Will you roll it for me?' Tagi asked him. 'My son always rolls mine for me.'

The boy knew that he was lying but he understood why.

'Certainly,' he said. Tagi handed him the cigarette paper.

'How can one so young like you roll cigarettes?' he asked.

'Samasoni taught me,' the boy said, as he deftly rolled the cigarette.

'He insisted that I teach him,' said Samasoni. 'Your mother doesn't know, does she?' The boy shook his head. He licked the cigarette and handed it to Tagi.

'I hope not,' said the old man, trying to look stern. 'Or she'll come over here and tell us off.' He threw the boy a box of matches.

The boy lit a match, using only one hand.

'You're a clever fellow,' Tagi remarked, taking a deep puff on his cigarette. The boy blushed. He liked people to tell him he was clever.

'I can smoke too!' he said proudly. The man laughed.

'If your grandmother ever finds out, we're for it,' said Samasoni.

'I don't care,' replied the boy. 'Grandmother lets me roll her smokes for her!'

As the water whirled lazily around his feet, the boy sat and watched Tagi smoking. Every puff seemed to count, all important. A fuia flew overhead and relieved the blue monotony of the sky; its dark reflection was trapped in the water for a brief moment and then was gone forever. The boy saw Tagi shudder. The others remained silent. The old man stood up as if the freedom of the fuia had reminded him of something, and muttered:

'I'll be back soon.'

The boy watched him leave with the sunlight dancing on his grey hair. The prison gates clanged from far off. The boy saw a smile blossom across Samasoni's face.

'Be out soon,' he heard Samasoni sigh.

'Where are you from, Tagi?' he asked.

'Falefa,' Tagi whispered, his eyes gazing far away.

'Oh, that's right,' blurted the boy, 'someone was telling us . . . . ' He stopped: Samasoni had motioned to him to keep quiet. The boy glanced at Tagi, who was picking at the wounds on his hand. He hadn't heard. The boy jumped up, picked up a stone and hurled it into the stream, watching it cleave the water and send wavelets to both banks. He whooped like an Indian.

'What are you doing here?' a fierce voice asked him.

He wheeled, and relaxed when he saw who it was. It was the fat police sergeant. Beside him stood the old man.

'Have you come?' he greeted the policeman. The policeman smiled and tweaked him under the chin. The boy punched him playfully in the stomach. And together they went into boxing stances.

'C'mon,' challenged the policeman, trying to hold in his large paunch. 'Hit me!'

The boy threw a left, he missed and felt a gentle tap on his cheek.

'Ha!' laughed his fat opponent. 'Put up that guard!' The boy threw another left, followed by a right to the stomach. The policeman feinted the left but the right landed.

'Ufff!' cried the policeman, pretending he was winded. The boy dropped his guard. The policeman slapped him gently on the cheek. 'I fooled you.' They laughed and the boy ran and sat down beside Tagi, who had opened his Bible and was reading it.

'What are we having for lunch?' the policeman asked. None of the prisoners replied.

'Breadfruit and fish,' said the boy.

'Good, good,' said the policeman, trying to smile at everyone. 'Can I see you for a minute?' he asked the old man. The old man followed him. The policeman stopped as if he had forgotten something. He turned to Tagi and said, 'Are you alright?' Tagi nodded. 'Is there anything you need?' Tagi shook his head slowly. The policeman turned and walked away.

Instinctively, the boy concluded that what was wrong had something to do with Tagi. Everyone was treating him delicately as if they were feeling guilty about something. The boy gazed at Tagi. The man's hair seemed to be growing whiter. He blinked.

'Will you put a tattoo on my hand?' he asked Tagi. 'I want a star.' Tagi looked at him. 'Please, will you, Tagi?' he repeated.

Samasoni stopped working and said, 'Why don't you, Tagi. The meal won't be ready for a while yet.' Tagi nodded.

Samasoni got up and hurried to the jail and his cell to get the soot and needles.

'It'll hurt a lot,' Tagi warned him, after closing the Bible and placing it on a rock.

'I can take it,' said the boy. 'I want the star right here.' He pointed at the space between his thumb and forefinger.

Tagi smiled and dabbed his eyes with the end of his lavalava.

The boy looked up and saw the old man standing in front of them. Holding out a tin of corned beef to Tagi, the old man said, 'It's for you from the policeman who was here.' Tagi accepted the tin.

'Tagi's going to put a star on my hand,' the boy told the old man.

They didn't say anything more while they waited for

Samasoni. The boy looked at the water. He leaned over and played with his reflection. Then he noticed something funny. Tagi's reflection seemed to be disappearing. He reached over and touched Tagi's shoulder in an attempt to re-establish the fact that Tagi was still there next to him.

Samasoni came stamping into the compound like a dark bull and handed Tagi the needles and soot. 'It's going to hurt,' he laughed at the boy.

The boy extended his hand. Tagi held it firmly. The boy relaxed – the man's hand felt like his mother's.

'Clench it tightly,' Tagi instructed him. Then dipping the needles in the watered soot he drew the outline of a star on the back of the boy's hand. No one spoke.

The boy felt the first pain shoot up his arm as the needle punctured the skin of his hand. And he closed his eyes, his face set in a grimace. As the jabbing continued, the pain grew duller. The boy opened his eyes. Tagi smiled sheepishly at him. The boy looked down at his hand. Blood was oozing from the tattoo like red paste. Tagi wiped the blood off with a wet cloth. One black line was finished.

'Do you want me to go on?' Tagi asked him. The boy nodded. The needles continued to make pain, and his hand became numb. A short while later, when he opened his eyes, a black cross stared at him from his hand.

He glanced at Tagi and asked, 'How much more?'

'Not long now. Be brave,' encouraged the man.

The youth sped into the compound. The boy saw him halt behind Tagi.

'Tagi, your family want to see you now,' the youth said and wheeled and left again.

Tagi stopped tattooing and looked at the boy.

'You'd better go now,' the boy told him. 'You can finish it later.'

The man staggered up slowly, picked up his Bible, brushed the dirt off it, and started walking away. The boy tried caressing the pain away from his hand. He looked up and saw that Tagi was looking back at him. He waved. Tagi waved back.

'Goodbye, Tagi!' he called, knowing that the man was not returning. He watched the disappearing figure of Tagi – a

19

hunched up man stumbling over the dry soil toward the corner of the jail, leaving only a faint trail of rising dust; and like the turning up of the palm of a hand Tagi disappeared around the jail.

The boy sat for a long time clutching his hand as though he was holding something precious. And as the sun dropped from noon shadows threw themselves like nets over him.

Samasoni and the old man worked on, now and then glancing at the boy. There was nothing they could do to help him.

Finally, as if in a daze, the boy got up and whispered, 'I'm going home now.' The two men nodded. The boy turned, waded through the taro plants, snaked himself under the wire fence and crossed over the steel pipe like a tightrope walker.

He paused on the other side and looked back as if he had forgotten something – as if he had crossed from one world to another, from one age to the next.

He found his mother squatting before a fire of embers, cooking fish. He walked up and stood behind her broad back.

'Who was the Man who died on the cross?'

His mother turned round. 'Where have you been?' she asked. The boy ignored her question and asked:

'Who was the Man who was crucified?'

'Why, Jesus,' replied his mother, staring questioningly at him. 'What's wrong? What's wrong with your hand?'

'Nothing,' he murmured.

'Then why are you holding it like that for?' She clutched his hand and turned it over. 'Who put that on your hand?' She was almost shouting.

'It's a cross,' he whispered. 'A man put it on.'

'What man?' she asked, noting with interest that for the first time her son was no longer afraid to stare straight at her when she was angry with him. He had changed, grown up.

'What man?' she asked. She wasn't angry anymore.

'Jesus,' he replied, examining the tattoo on his hand. 'And he's never coming back. Never. He left me only this.' He held up his hand, proudly.

# Captain Full —
# the Strongest Man Alive who got Allthing Strong Men got

Mine neighbourhood I to you must tell about. It lie like old woman who got no teeth between big Catholic Church and Police Station. There lie behind it swamp where the mosquito live like mad. There lie in front of it main street of town, Apia. There run through it stream-water call 'Vaipe' (mean dead-water). In mine neighbourhood you buy strong home-brew beer drive man crazy-mad. It also got woman and allthing men want to have bad – but this not mean mine neighbourhood evil sinful bad. It not. How it sinful be? It have got Church on other side, it got Police on other. If you sin Church put you right or Police put you right path again. If they no do you good you go die in swamp or drown in deep sea. Some people they do this but I no understand why they want give up living. Maybe they want bad go heaven early. I not know. I just simple man who no think deep too much. I like mine neighbourhood. I born there, grew up there, live dead middle of it. She mine neighbourhood is mother of me. Mine father now dead. I not know who mine mother is. Old women tell me mine mother she go heaven long time ago. Now she with God. So everynight before I go sleep I pray hard for she and mine father too. I tell God look after they like loving father look after child of him – I saintman church-going strong. I pray for all people who gone join angel-choir. I pray too for those alive still who need help bad cause they losing soul fast to devil. But I no want stress this cause I not boasting man. I modest. That why people like me.

Now I finish describe mine neighbourhood and all that,

I go tell about best friend of mine who now gone to meet his Maker seven year ago. His name Captain Full (I no want tell his real name cause afraid Devil from heaven drive him out). Captain Full he best barber in whole island even though he short ugly with one leg shortshort than other leg of him. Captain Full been marry four time – now he gone leave behind children number eighteen in all. This what other people think but I know Captain have eight other children from women he no marry to. Captain Full he real rooster.

First time I see Captain Full when I only fourteen year old. One day in marketplace mine friend come tell me quick that new barber come neighbourhood. They laugh alltime. They make me curious so I say: Why you fool laugh? And they say back: He most ugly man like small dog want weewee bad! Him like rooster got no feather on. I say nothing back. Then they say: They say he best barber-man in whole island. So I say: We go see him. So we go fast, hide behind fence and watch. (Captain Full he buy chinaman shop and make it his barber business) . . . . When Captain come out I laugh too. He most ugly man got glasses wear. And he walk like sick sick man got bad disease. Mine friend they run out and yell loud at he, Roosterman why you got ugliness? Why you short leg got? I nice boy I not join them for to tease Captain Full. Captain he look mad but he just walk by say no thing to mine friend who go tease him alltime.

Next day we come back and mine friend they do same tease. One boy he pick up stone and throw it at shop of Captain Full who come limp out and shake fist at us. But he can run no fast for to catch us. One day we get too bold walk right up and stand in door of shop. Then before knew I, Captain Full got me by neck, stretch me out and beat me bad. I cry real loud and yell, He killing me! He murderer! This scare Captain for to let me go. I stand up. Then see I he smile at me and I know he no longer have anger left then. Captain Full and me we now got friendship. So I ask him for to give me good haircut. And he done that and no ask me pay him. It best haircut I in mine whole life have. Captain Full talk alltime. He most talkest man I ever know. Just like volcano he talk – smooth talk rough talk anykind of talk. God give him this real-worth gift. God give him mouth of gold. That why we call him Captain Full – he full of talk. At first we call him Captain Full of Talktalk. But it too long so we cut it short to Captain Full. Even though Captain he talk alltime he never talk you about womenfolk. Best lovelife he have but he never talk about it. He no boasting man. Cause we young we talk alltime about makefire to girl. But Captain he never do this. Maybe he have too much already, and he real master of skirt game. Even American bigshot men who come on boat and I see take girl, talktalk alltime about their lovelife. But I know it cause they no real master of game like Captain Full. They make in word what they not done for real.

One day I pick up American bigshot who no want be with girl he want be with me. I shock bad. I not know what to do cause it first time one he want makefire with other he. This shock me so I go rush away leave bigshot there under tree with his fly open. I run to Captain and tell him allthing that happen. He just laugh and laugh and say: He queer, he halfgirl and you best stay clear of him. I then feel good again so I leave and go tell mine friend. They amaze. They say but why you not do this thing he ask he pay you big dollar. I turn and leave they. I know some of them done it with halfgirl bigshot for dollar and they sin bad. And it make me scare for it not natural-like for to do it with other he. Captain Full he tell me this, and I believe him.

One morning I visit Captain and find shop of him full up with children. They his children and they eighteen in all. I amaze. Captain Full he polite man he introduce me all round. Then he tell them go home. When shop all clear I say, God, you real man. Captain Full he just laugh and say: I got marry four time. That the result! He warn me not get marry when I grow up. Too much trouble and worry he say. So I make up mind right there I no marry. Captain he know best. When I tell him I not get marry he laugh and say: Wait boy, they get you like they go get me. (But he no fool me. It not the women who go got him it Captain who done all courting.) Then he sit me down on chair and give me hot haircut for free. Captain he alltime do this for me. He mine friend. He even start teach me how to be good barber like him and he allow me for to cut hair of children. He tell me I make real hot barber – I got talent he say.

As time go by I even start talktalk like Captain Full. He train me good. He teach me how to talk to girl and win she. He tell me, Now first thing you do you tell she you love she with all your heart. Tell her real smooth he say, so she no suspect you tell her lie. Then after you know she real warm on you, you tell she that she got to prove she love you back. How? she reply. Then you say, We makefire real quick. If she no agree you say, Then I go leave you for you no love me back. This make she cry, make her sad so sad for the thought she go lose you that she go agree do allthing you tell she do. Then Captain just laugh and laugh and say: But you go to wait for you only small fly with no bigstand yet. So I wait. I obey Captain for he know best, he master of game.

Now in mine neighbourhood there live woman called Fanua. (I no tell her real name cause the Police they after her alltime.) Fanua she mine friend cause I bring her many American bigshot with big dollar. Fanua she real game, real female master of game. She got big heart love everybody and she never hurt a fly. She one time daughter of strong-church-going pastor. And she have real education in college, in college where they teach girl to be good wife for young pastor. So you see Fanua she not ignorant like most people in mine neighbourhood. She educated. But she came real gone on worthless fellow who got no heart and only want one thing with she. Fanua she too in love for to see this and she give it to him who no love her back. And he give her girl-child who is nighttime offspring and he no marry her. Then her father he chase her out of home. Now she use English she learn in college for to get dollar off American bigshot. I give her name Fanua cause she a lady like the earth and she like a mother to me. Now Fanua she real big woman got allthing in right place and go willing at right time for right dollar value.

One day she happen go past barber shop. I run out and talk with she. As she walk away I glance see Captain Full stand there like a man near go drown. And I know he gone on Fanua. So I say, You like she? Captain Full he just laugh but it unsure laugh like laugh of man who got lost his way in jungle. He say nothing but I know he far gone on Fanua.

That night I go visit Fanua and say there is friend of mine who want see her but she not for to make this obvious when she go see him. When I tell her it the barber Captain Full she just laugh and laugh and say, Him? But he so ugly and small. He never able for to make me laugh! You wait see I say to she, I bet you die in bed with he! This make her real curious. (Fanua she always curious bad everytime I tell her this man real hot stick.) So I leave her. I know tomorrow she go find out if Captain Full hot like I tell her.

Next day I go early to Captain Full and work as barber, say nothing to him. Alltime I looksee if Fanua is to come. When I see her come float like dream toward shop I leave say nothing to Captain. Fanua she all dressup in silk dress and she have on her yellow shoe and necklace. She really a dream. I wave to she and run to marketplace.

When I return two hour later she still there sit in barber chair. I down heart sudden for it obvious nothing happen between she and Captain. The Captain he just stand there like lost boy say nothing. Fanua give him eye alltime but Captain he no respond, he no longer master of game. So I make mind up quick and say, Fanua you got real hot shoe on. Eh, Captain? Captain just nod his head and look at floor. She got real hot dress. Eh Captain? I say again. Fanua just laugh and say, Don't try too hard boy. The Captain he no Captain nomore. He little boy lost! I look at Captain, hope he say something. But he look hurt, say nothing. So I turn and leave again, hope he gain control of game.

When I return the door of shop it shut so I go to back of shop and peep through crack in wall. The Captain stand there, he no shirt have on and Fanua she giggle and begin pull off his lavalava. Fanua she now real master of game. The Captain he lost little boy like Fanua say. But it working so I leave run home alltime smile to self. I happy it working fine between Fanua and Captain cause they both best friend of mine. I pass church – stand there white like bare backside of horse we have once – but I nomore afraid if it call me sinnerman. That not matter now cause Fanua and Captain they good people. And it no matter if church say it allwrong for to bedfire outside of marryingbusiness. The Church it don't exist now. The Police it don't exist. Cause there only Captain and Fanua meet for first time and nothing else matter to them except themself. They become one as preacher say. I stop and look at swamp lie there like dead smelly man and I go scare and remember sudden that mine father die there cause priest tell him he commit sin when he makefire with wife of other man. And he sin bad cause he drink too much and beat up this woman till she go to hospital and die there. Mine father go kill himself there in swamp. I look at sea, it lie there like hungry shark it wait for me so I run fast. Allthing round me they no like me they wait for me. I so scare when I look see Police station. It stand there and it remind of day when mine brother die there in cell – the Police they beat him till he die. I pick up rock and throw it hard at jail then I run home fast like man got ghost after him.

That night I no go sleep. Nightmare they haunt me. I go scare so I pray hard to Father-in-Heaven tell him look after mine father and mine mother and mine brother. They not live long but they all try hard to live best way they know how to live. And God he answer me for he make me sleep and dream nice dream about Captain Full and Fanua. They want to live too like mine father mother and brother want to live. I wake quick. I know the swamp Church sea and Police they all wait for Fanua and Captain and me. But they not going for to get me! I say to me. No they not going for to get me!

When the sun high like fat hen I go fast to Captain Full. When I arrive he there whistling alltime. He so happy I see. While he work he keep laugh to himself and I know why – Fanua she real good to him. I no ask though. I polite boy. Two friend of mine arrive soon. They want me go with them cause there big ship in harbour with plenty American bigshot. But I tell them no and they go by themself. Soon Fanua come walkby. I look at she. She walk like she go for to meet her Maker, like she really satisfy with life. It first time she

look like this. And I know why and I so happy. I no hear
what they speak about. Fanua she leave soon but I know she
be back soon to see Captain.

Soon she back. And I see Captain all sudden go unhappy
most unhappiest man alive right then. He sing nomore but
watch as she go by. Fanua she have American bigshot follow
her like pet dog who want release pretty bad – I know then
she go to earn some dollar. I unhappy for Captain but I
know I cannot do anything for to make him smile again.
Anyway I say to me she got to earn living best way she
know how. It her job. She don't love bigshot. But Captain
Full he no see this reason, he too far gone on she.

In afternoon when the sun so hot it feel like madness
Fanua return. When I see her stand in doorway I get up
and leave. She give me shilling when I go past she. I curious
for to see what Captain do to she so I duck to back of shop
and watchsee through crack in wall. The Captain I see he
hit her hard sudden. She start cry and say, But it my job, I
earn money! The Captain grab her hair and tell her: You
a whore! Fanua cry hard and ask him for to forgive her.
Then Captain go soft all sudden and forgive she. He kiss
her allover. Then she close her eye lie back on mat and pull
her skirt up. I no want see nomore cause God watch me
and know I sinning bad for it not good boy who sit there and
watch bad thing like that. But I no can close mine eyes. I
stare alltime feel hot allover. Fanua peep up at Captain and
she smile and reach up and pull down he to she. Then I
looksee up to heaven ask God forgive me for I sin bad.
But I no see God upthere. I go get scare for all sudden I
want so bad for to play with me. But I slap me and stand up
and flee. The Captain and Fanua they good people and it
hurt them bad if they know I watch. I run hard and stand
on edge of sea. The wave they come in like men who got
anger bad. The wind it whisper to me, YOU BAD! YOU
BAD! YOU SIN AND I NOT HIDE YOU FROM SIN!
It have voice of priest and I start cry for I go scare and feel
all alone with me. No one there for to help me. No one
to come and say, I HELP YOU BOY. YES, I HELP YOU!
I now alone. Gradual-like I know I got to live with me
even though there no one there for to help me, be with me

like father. So I sing and sing, try hard to live with me, save
me. AND I DID. I sudden feel no scare nomore. I by myself
but I no afraid nomore. I no scare of priest or God or
anything. For the sea change to peace and the sky it float
upthere like mother of me. They all sudden become part of
me. They all hide me from eye of God. And mine father
mother and brother they no can see me for allthing hide me.
I sing and sing and dance and dance. People pass me they
think I gone mad. But I no care about them. They no harm
me cause I no longer afraid of anything. There for me
nomore evil or good. These thing they nomore exist for me.
I above allthing. I NOW ME! I NOW FREE CAN DO
ALLTHING, NO GUILT FEEL NOMORE!

Mine friend they come and find me there full of strength.
They no say anything for they know I change complete.
Tomorrow, I say to them, you come with me. I got surprise
for you but you got to pay me shilling each. They all agree
for they know me – they know I no tell lie I make it worth-
while for them to see. (One time Captain he tell me that any
man can do anything he like if he free man if he himself. I
now free so I can anything do.)

Next day when I see Fanua arrive for the Captain to see
I go out quick and take mine friend behind shop. There five
of them. I collect shilling for each and give them long hot
peep. Boy, they cry like they gone mad – Boy, watch him!
Boy, watch her cry! I no say anything I sit there hold tight
to five shilling mine friend give me. Boy, they say, Captain
Full he real good stick like no man I ever seen! When session
over mine friend they sit they all feel weak they want real
bad be in place of Captain for they all still virgin. Tomorrow
it cost you two shilling each I tell they. They all agree quick.
So for two week I make plenty money. And God he no
disturb me he too far away for to worry me.

Every night mine friend I meet. And I talk with them like I
is Captain Full. Captain he teach me good. I now came
smooth talker like him. I describe allthing to mine friend
even give them real lie but they no see. They all dumb virgin.
I virgin too but I no tell them this.

Now in mine neighbourhood there live Solo. He older
than me and he no talk much. He like giant spider him tall

and dark and look like big spider. He a poetman cause he spin web of poetword. It happen one night as I talk to mine friend Solo he come along and listen to me. When I finish tale of me seduce virgin girl he just laugh and laugh and say, Your friend he coming like Captain Full. He getting full of talktalk. I get mad sudden for he tell truth and I no want him tell mine friend that I tell lie. Why you say I a liar? I yell to him. Solo he just laugh and say: But you lie. You know you lie, fly! I bit scare of Solo. I once see him beat up big man beat him so bad the man he got broken jaw. So I no want fight Solo for he beat me for sure and I try and laugh and say, You want me prove it? Solo nod his head and mine friend nod their head too they all want me prove mine talk. I lost all sudden. I not know what to do for I still virgin. You prove it with first skirt who come by, fly! Solo order me. He mean it and I so scare I want flee away from him. But I know I can no run away for Solo catch me quick and beat me. If I flee I lose mine friend too. I brave boy and I go through with it I whisper to me. So we wait and sit. No one come this time of night I tell them. But Solo he just smile and tell me waitsee. I feel like I turn to stone.

Two young girl come along road and sit front of market-place. Go to it, fly! Solo order me. (I scare when he call me fly cause he like a spider, and spider it eat the fly.) I go get up slow feel knee weak and walk over to girl, hope they leave before I arrive. But they no leave. Then I think of what Captain tell me and all sudden say to me: You can do it boy. Be easy! (This make me feel bit brave.)

I just walk up and sit down between the two girl. They giggle. But I know I handsome like Errol Flynn, can do the deed. I never seen girl before. I hope they not strongchurch-goer for they the hardest to make with so Captain tell me. Strongchurchgoer girl they strong believer in virgin-business.

What your name? I say. They not tell me. Where you from? They no tell me. They both older than me but I big as they. One girl she ugly bad the other she not bad looker. This one give me eye alltime so I make up mine mind. Solo and mine friend come and hide and watch me work. Would you like icecream? I ask the girl. They giggle and nod head. I give ugly one two shilling tell her go to chinaman and get icecream. She laugh and go. It working boy I tell me. Now work quick.

You good looker, I whisper soft to she. She giggle and say, You not bad too. I push up close feel her skin hot to me. (The Captain train me good. I never do this before but I do it now do everything right like Captain tell me do.) I look at sky search for moon. But there no moon so I no can say to she, You real beauty like the moon. I look at sea but it too dark for to see it so I can no say to she, You beauty like the sea. I lost for something to say. I sit there like dead rock. But she save me. She break strain when she say, Why not we go and sit under tree over there? She take mine hand and lead me like a baby to dark under tree. I hear other friend of mine follow quiet. I not doing anything she doing it and make me feel like fool. But I no care. Solo he not know this he think it me who persuade she.

We sit under tree and look at sea. Why you shy? she say to me. I love you I reply quick. Then I know I say the wrong thing for she laugh all sudden and say, Boy, you real hot liar! But I no tell lie I say, You beauty girl and I love you. Then she move like octopus and swamp me. I no show have (I know Solo watch real close. I have to make thing look like I the one who win she not she win me.) I hold her close-tight like second skin and turn her over. She help me fast. Before I know I no lavalava have and her lavalava it way up on her face. I got scare fast. I not know what to do next. What the matter? she pant, why you not strong? She clutch I but I still no grow strong. Oh, she giggle, you virgin eh? She make me ashame. This make me want for to hit she. I fall hard on to she. And all sudden she say: Boy you big! Boy you big! I no scare nomore then for I know I as good as Captain Full. And real quick I be in she all hot with she. All sudden I no longer lost virgin. (Boy I no tell lie. Allthing I describe they true like it happen.) I feel like I being swallowed up like Jonah in belly of whale. I feel like King in heaven like I chief who own all female on earth. And I stabstab at she like I on fire and she allround me like earth sky and sea. Then I find release. I real flow quick into

30

she and I cry loud like baby come out of motherwomb. And she hold me tight like I her own heart and she whisper, You good, boy! You good like noone I know before. I smile to me for I know then I better than Captain Full. I push she away from me. She no matter to me nomore and I feel I hate she for she not worthy for to take from me mine virgin-thing. I look up and see Solo stand there. He believe then. I get up slow and look real smart. I FOOL THEM ALL. BOY I FOOL THEM ALL! Solo he pat me on back and say: Sorry fly, you no tell lie! The girl she sit up quick and cover her nakedness. She ashame all sudden. But I no ashame. I A MAN NOW. I walk away with mine friend and they ask me: How was it? So I tell them all make them feel like schoolchildren. I look back. The girl she sit there like she going to cry and Solo stand over her. I not even know her name. But I no guilt feel. I no care. I see Solo he try to make she but she stand up fast and swear at him make him look a fool. I laugh to me. I not the fool – Solo he the fool now.

Week later I go see Captain Full. He just sit there in barber chair I see. Him near in tear and look sick and he no want to cut hair of people there. I say nothing to him. I pick up clipper and begin do barber job for him. (After all I his friend as I stress already.) When I finish I leave say nothing to him for I know he no want to speak about his trouble.

When I come back next day he not there. So I open shop and take control of his barber business. Customer who come ask me: Where Captain Full? I tell them he sick bad. They no care really if Captain not there cause I as good as Captain in barber business. They all begin for to call me Captain Full the Second. But soon I know they make name short to Captain Full. It good they do this I feel for I proving I a better man than Captain Full.

For long time Captain he no come to shop. And I take over allthing. Fanua she no appear too. Then one afternoon when it hot like fire in hell Captain Full appear sudden. He most sickest man I ever seen. He so thin you break him easy. He cough alltime and he yellow colour like old chinaman. He come and stand in doorway – there he stare at me. I not turn to him. I continue cut hair of boy in barber chair. But alltime I feel he angry with me. Captain Full stand there till all customer go then he break out to me.

What you do eh? You steal mine shop! He yell at me. I smile at him for he too weak for to harm me I bigger than him. You done it to me! he cry loud. You done it to me! What I done? I ask. I getting angry too. You bring along me to Fanua. You got she to makefire with me cause you want mine shop! You get she for to give me disease so I go sick and you get mine shop! He yell at me. He jump at me and begin strangle me. But I strong I push him away and say to him: You lie it not mine fault. I no tell you go fall in love with Fanua. I never tell you go makefire with she! Captain he sob hard and the tear come like water from his eye. He cry and cry but he no weaken me.

You lie! You lie! he cry. Fanua she give me bad disease. You tell she do it to me! What disease? I ask him. She give me firewood! he cry. I going to die cause it got me bad. It eating me! He stare at me ask me for to save him. But I nomore feel anything for him. It his own fault he sick with firewood disease. I no care about weak people. Only strong people have the right for to live and I one of the strong people. Captain he the one who tell me all this – it him who make me believe this it him who change me so it his fault I no feel anything for him. I say nothing to him. If he die he die. It his fault. Captain Full he turn slow and leave shop like old man. I turn and stare close at mine picture in mirror and I pick up the comb and comb the hair. I now the real Captain Full and there nothing else in mirror but me.

Two month later Captain Full die. Firewood disease got him bad eat him up slow. No one blame me. They all blame Captain himself. He lead sinful life they say that why he die bad death – it God's will, God punish those who sin against his commandment.

I now own shop of Captain Full. (I know he want me to for I best barber in whole island and I his friend who pray for him.) I own two other shop too. People they astound cause I so young. They say it God's blessing for I a good man who love religion. And it God's way for to give richness to those who follow him. The people they now call me

Captain Full but I not going to die like Captain Full who now in heaven. I Captain Full but I not sinful. I stay clear of girl who got firewood disease. I now also control women-business in mine neighbourhood. Fanua and four other girl they all work for me. All mine friend also work for me. I STRONGEST MAN ALIVE. Soon I control all business in mine neighbourhood. Captain Full he teach me good. But he only small man who had no big plan like me. I got power now even Police leave me alone. I not even afraid of God anymore. Why I be afraid of God? It him who bless me with all mine richness. The priest he don't worry me. Last week I give him big cheque for to help his school. He thank me and say he going to pray for me. The swamp the sea they not going for to get me. When I get big dollar I going to buy the swamp suck out the water and turn it to good land for to build new part of town. I A MAN WHO BELIEVE IN PROGRESS. I also going to leave mine neighbourhood. I going to live up on side of mountain in big European house. I not married yet but I got mine eye on daughter of pastor. This girl she virgin for sure and it all good men who got religion who marry virgin. This God's will.

All this I gone and said are true. It all happen like I say. I no tell you lie for I the strongest man alive who is strong believer in truth and who got allthing strong men got. God he on mine side and this side is right side. If mine father mother brother and Captain Full see me now they all be proud of me.

# Pint-size Devil
# on a Thoroughbred

After a meal of steak and eggs, I gave him a pound note –
not because I had believed his story about needing the
money to buy schoolbooks for his children, but because,
after nearly a week, I wanted him to leave and I had, as
usual, enjoyed his performance: the flattery, the child-like
darting eyes, the instant tears, the imaginary aches and pains
in his arms and legs, his complete disbelief in God, Whom
he constantly called down as his witness to the 'truth' of his
stories, and his astoundingly detailed knowledge of our
family history. Yes, against my wife's advice I gave him
a pound, and Pili, who was an uncle by adoption (my
grandparents had done the adopting over fifty years before),
journeyed to Apia in a taxi, and after losing nearly the whole
pound at billiards, had 'carnal knowledge', so the Judge
later said, of a knowledgeable fourteen-year-old girl behind
the Mulivai Cathedral, was caught while increasing his
knowledge and, after a short trial during which Pili never
once told the truth, was sentenced to nine months hard
labour in Tafaigata Prison – an institution not alien to Pili
who had already spent well over nine years there, before.
The following is an outline of his major prison sentences: in
1935, six months for stealing and eating a neighbour's
prize boar; in 1938, one year for helping some friends beat
up and rob two foreign sailors who had already paid ten
dollars apiece to lay two girls whom he had procured for
them; in 1947, two years for forging a £100 cheque, using
my father's signature, and gambling away all of it in a poker
game which he had organised and which had lasted for three

days; in 1950, one and a half years for inciting a riot in a well-known and respected Chinese merchant's store, such riot resulting in £500 worth of damage – the merchant's half-caste wife having called Pili a 'dirty mongrel son of a coolie', her statement containing some element of truth because Pili's real father was full-blooded Chinese; in 1954, after three poverty-stricken years of going straight, two years for helping some friends help themselves to £200/13/2, plus two rolls of red silk, ten cartons of cigarettes, and three packets of chewing gum, which didn't belong to them; and, in 1960, one year for absconding with church funds belonging to a village in Savaii.

My whole family (and just about everyone I know) will tell you that Pili was born with the Devil in his heart, anger in his brain, and a goat in his loins. His criminal record, which fills a whole drawer in the Police Department, seems to support such a view. The numerous women, whom he used for the siring of numerous children (outside the church) and as a source of food, money and free sex, would also, if called upon, bear witness to his 'inherent badness' (a phrase used by Judge Macarthy in Pili's last trial). So would all the people, things, and animals he had robbed or assaulted or conned. So would the Police. And my wife. But what they won't admit to you is this: Pili had style, polish, manners; he was completely suited to the role of robbing, cuckolding and beating us up, of plundering our daughters' cherries, and generally acting as our spiritual flail.

Pili was a little over five feet in height and built like a jockey; in fact, in his early twenties he had been a jockey but had been suspended for life after crowding the favourite horse and its rider against the inside rail, causing the horse to break its neck, and the jockey his spine. The horse had to be shot (Pili even offered to pull the trigger) and the jockey, who was, according to Pili, a chicken-hearted amateur who by being what he was had *forced* him to do what he had done, had to retire for life as a twenty-one-year-old cripple. Pili's racing career was absolutely without sportsmanship and gallantry; he had to win every race, and anyone – apprentice jockeys, veteran jockeys, managers, trainers and officials – who threatened his chances had to be eliminated. After all, he needed the money, every penny of it, to play poker and women, his two passions in life. He had no love for horses, whatsoever – at least that's what everyone has told me. He didn't know, or want to know, anything about horses, either. A horse was a horse, a four-footed speed-machine which, for the jockey's sake, had to be whipped, if need be, to the finishing line ahead of other speed-machines. Most of the trainers and owners knew this, yet they all wanted Pili to ride their horses because Pili was the sure thing, a winner, a jockey who could, overnight, increase one's reputation as a gentleman owner-trainer of winning speed-machines. Horse-racing, to most of the merchants who own most of the race-horses in my country, is not for making a fast pound; it isn't business, it's strictly for pleasure, cultured fun, something to enhance one's reputation as a successful merchant who has no interest whatsoever in making money anymore, as a gentleman, a cultured European (whether part-Chinese, part-European, part anything) fifteen cuts above the 'natives'. To hell with the money.

Pili rode winners for them, earned them gentlemanly reputations and, for himself a 'native', the reputation as the dirtiest jockey on the track, the pint-size devil on a thorough-bred. But when he broke the neck of that horse (nevermind the 'native' jockey) which belonged to Mr Asheley and Son Ltd, the Racing Association suspended him forever. The Association, I should mention, was chaired by Mr Asheley who was also Chairman of the Chamber of Commerce, Chairman of the R.S.A., Chairman of the English-speaking Protestant Church, a European Member of Parliament; or, in other words, the richest self-made, self-taught European (part-American) son of a beach-comber in the country.

A week later, during an early morning practice at the race track, Pili provoked a fight with Asheley's son who was over six feet tall and weighed a solid 200 pounds but who was a gentleman who forgot that Pili wasn't a gentleman. Within one short brutal round Pili upper-kicked him between the legs and, while Asheley's son lay on the muddy ground groaning and clutching his genitals, Pili sculptured his handsome face with swift professional strokes of his feet. Being a gentleman – he had been to one of the most exclusive boarding schools in New Zealand and later to university where he failed to begin a commercial degree – Asheley's son brought charges of assault and battery against Pili. But the witnesses, mainly Pili's jockey friends who were too scared of Pili to be anything else but friendly, witnessed in Court that 'Mister Asheley's Son' – everyone called him that – had started the fight by hitting Pili (who was after all a defenceless dwarf compared to his giant victim) with his riding whip, for no reason at all. What they didn't tell the Judge was what they had heard Pili say to 'Mister Asheley's Son' before the fight: 'Your expensive horse's balls are as big as your father's cheap ones'. What the Judge didn't know either was the fact that Pili had been Bantam-Weight Boxing Champion of Western Samoa two years before.

Pili was almost illiterate, but he had a genuine respect for education. He could sign his name (and my father's) to cheques and pay sheets, count his money (and everyone else's) to a penny, and expertly read playing cards, dice and what other people were thinking or were likely to think and do. Pili was an expert in his own field – at what he wanted to master, manipulate, and put to profitable use. Not that he would have analysed his gift along these lines. He would have laughed if I had ever told him this, and would have 'modestly' called himself:

> An ignorant fool
> Who never went to school

According to my father, my grandfather was largely responsible for the way Pili turned out and for his lack of formal education. My grandfather was a high chief at our village, and a product, so I've been told, of the old *pagan* school. He was dictatorial, to the point of physically assaulting anyone who opposed his wishes; arrogant, to the almost insufferable degree of calling himself 'King of the District' (and, when drunk, which wasn't often after he married grandmother, the 'King of Samoa'); politically

ambitous, to the heights of manoeuvring, like a second
Machiavelli, to grab any matai title to which he was
intimately or remotely connected; verbally brilliant, to the
ridiculous limits of sophistry, dazzling listeners with his
highly poetic oratory about any topic under the moon in
the cause of increasing his reputation as an orator par
excellence; just, to the full meaning of that word as he saw
it, meting out instant justice according to what he and no
one else (not even the law) believed was right and wrong;
proud, to the sky of unforgiveness – my grandmother
claims that grandfather never forgot an insult, or what he
thought was an insult, no matter how slight it was and
sometimes planned and waited for years to have his revenge;
physically strong, fit, and fast with his fists, a quality which
not many men forgot after grandfather, fifteen years older
and much lighter than the Chief of Police, reduced that
Chief, who was the most feared man in town, to a bloody,
scarred-for-life, one-week-unconscious mess (the Police
Chief had jailed Pili for two days for giving cheek to some of
his policemen); a Christian, only through an accident in
history – everyone else in Samoa was a Christian, attending
church regularly – and was appointed a deacon, not because
the pastor considered him a devout Christian but because
grandfather *wanted* to be a deacon in *his* church, and
delivered sermons (whenever he felt the urge) which were
political and worldly to the point of heresy, always paid his
church dues, and was responsible for organising all church
projects in the village, was not noted for spiritual patience –
he could never tolerate long-winded sophisticated sermons
or prayers and would either go to sleep or get up and leave
the church, and was not particularly spiritual in his humour,
preferring to tell outrageous, bawdy and lusty yarns of his
own peculiar invention during the pastor's Sunday dinners;
a grand fisherman, sometimes going well beyond the reef
in a canoe and returning with mullet, bonito, barracuda,
and shark; abhorred plantation work so much that if it
hadn't been for grandmother's managerial skill our family
would have eaten only fish and more fish – he claimed that
trees were made by the Almighty not to be cut down but to
decorate and clothe the earth's nakedness, and, when picked

on by grandmother for being lazy, would yell: 'God can damn well take care of the crops Himself!'; was the most famous traditional dancer our village has ever produced, and one who was not reluctant to boast about it, ordering male dancers, whom he called 'women', off the dance-floor during important district feasts and meetings, and then demonstrating how the siva should be performed.

Apart from grandmother I don't think grandfather respected women, or let's say, he treated them as infuriating pets, bearers of male heirs, workers on the plantation, cooks, drawers of water and hewers of wood who should never be treated as political let alone social equals. The role he permitted women was one which had been completely acceptable to both the pre-European Samoan male and female, but a role which has become neurotically unacceptable to most modern Samoan women and a few Samoan males.

Grandfather looked upon papalagi as beings to be tolerated because of their superior knowledge of machines (especially guns) and food (especially ice-cream which was grandfather's favourite food). Otherwise, they were inferior in their arrogance; childish in their preoccupation with what they called 'conscience'; completely without breeding and manners; physically weak and emotionally warped, proof of the latter being their fanatical drive to manufacture weapons that would eventually destroy them; insane in their lifetime preoccupation with acquiring material wealth and security, and in their selfish individualism and self-chosen mission of enslaving superior races like the Samoans. The papalagi males were highly effeminate, a result of their relationship to their women and children. ('They allow their wives to boss them around, eat out their maleness – look at the way their wives make them wash the dishes, put on baby's nappies, clean up baby's shit', grandfather was fond of pointing out to grandmother. 'Their wives wear the pants, and they wear aprons!') Grandfather however could never rid himself of the annoying feeling of admiration which he had for certain missionaries, doctors, and teachers, especially the ones who knew and praised things Samoan. And because he didn't want to ever reveal this to anyone, he classed it as 'superstition'. Grandfather argued that, like ghosts, missionaries, doctors and teachers dealt primarily with things of the mind and heart and, like ghosts when riled, these beings could easily destroy one's sanity. It was far easier to cope with a papalagi who attacked you with a gun than with one who attacked you with an incomprehensible idea, who moulded your mind with appealing ideals and judgements, who showed you other ways that were compellingly attractive – ways that were beyond your familiar world contained in the reef of what you knew.

Grandfather was extremely superstitious, but, unlike most superstitious people, he wasn't really afraid of the supernatural. He accepted ghosts not as hostile beings who, divorced from his world were all the time planning to invade that world, but as beings who were part of his universe to be lived with as he had to live with other human beings and animals. After all, ghosts were at one time live beings of flesh and blood like you and me, he often told my family. If one was afraid of a ghost, he was only showing that he was afraid of another human being. And, as far as I've been able to find out, grandfather wasn't afraid of anything that was alive, whether visible or invisible, and on two feet, as it were. When my father, aunts and uncles were children mortally scared of the dark and the supernatural, grandfather, to prove that ghosts were only playful and harmless beings, often went into the nearest graveyard and there slept until morning on the biggest grave. Some nights, he'd forced his children to go with him. But to this day, my father, aunts and uncles are still afraid of the dark and ghosts; they try their best not to show it though, and have sought protection in Protestanism. I think I've inherited their weak streak, but, unlike them, I hide behind a mask of atheistic cynicism. Out of all my aunts and uncles, Pili was the only one who, like grandfather, found ghosts friendly and not conducive to insanity. I suppose this was one of the reasons why my family have grouped Pili with the ghostly legions of the damned. (He is dead now, but his ghost haunts my family like those ghosts that haunted them when they were children.) My Aunt Ita, the most devout inheritor of the Victorian brand of Christianity which the missionaries brought, having driven two pastor husbands to ulcer deaths and five children into the civil service, is a loquacious advocater of the theory that Pili was one-part ghost and three-parts criminal because, in his youth, grandfather took him too often to graveyards and fed him on the indigestible and fearful diet of ghosts. My Aunts Fatu and Alofa – the former a prodigious breeder, the latter a spinster, but who are both easily led – believe Aunt Ita's theory which has become, after Pili's lengthy criminal career, a 'tradition' among many of my family. Being weak-spined in relation to the supernatural, I too find the 'tradition' *attractive*, to admit the least.

Grandfather then was the person (or shall we say the 'elemental force') who can be blamed, if anyone or anything is to be blamed, for Pili becoming the 'pint-size devil on a thoroughbred'. Grandfather who was a remnant from the pre-Christian era, a law unto himself (and everybody else), and certainly not what papalagi adventurers, beachcombers, writers, poets, and tourists have called the 'Polynesian noble savage'. (If what I've written so far suggests, in any way, that he was a 'noble savage', then blame it on the giant-size yarn-neurosis from which all writers suffer. Grandfather would have laughed at what I've written, that is if he was able to read it. You see, grandfather couldn't read or write.) Pili, so to speak, became a jockey-sized version of grandfather, an embodiment of grandfather's worst characteristics. *Worst* because grandfather never intentionally used anyone for personal gain, or kicks, or from sheer malice. Pili existed and thrived outside the law, the Church, the conventional. He was, like grandfather, a law unto himself, but, unlike grandfather, a 'criminal' (to use a word most acceptable to the police, judges, and other self-styled law enforcers), a 'complete outsider' (to use a term more appealing to sociologists, liberals, psychiatrists, anthropologists, and the literati), or 'one of the Damned' (to borrow from fundamentalists, like my father, and evangelists, like my Uncle Solomona who is, apart from Pili, the only other person in my family who can con people on a large scale).

Because Pili was the youngest – he was ten years younger

41

than my youngest aunt – he was destined to become my grandparents' favourite, something which the elders in my family never forgave Pili for and something which my grandmother is still trying to say wasn't true. Pili was my grandmother's sister's son; his father was a Chinaman who came to Samoa as an indentured labourer sometime in the 1890s. Before Pili was born, his father, in a row which thrilled the whole neighbourhood, accused Pili's mother of adultery, the swelling in her adulterous womb being the result, so my grandparents decided to adopt the child when it was born. Grandfather, I think, had become disillusioned with the way his other sons had turned out. All meek and mild and spineless, he told grandmother. So he wanted to start anew with another son. My grandparents couldn't have any more children of their own, and it wasn't from the lack of trying on grandfather's part or the lack of prayers on grandmother's part. Grandfather wanted another son, another chance to try and create his ideal man – and what grandfather wanted, he got, Uncle Solomona will tell you with a self-righteous chuckle. Serves Papa right, Aunt Ita will echo. My father would simply stare at the ceiling, or at any other blank space near him, and be non-committal. Grandmother would get angry and threaten to reverse the birth process concerning the whole lot of them, and tell me, because she thinks I'm the most understanding man in the family, having a university degree to prove it, that grandfather was a 'good Christian'. And I'd side with her because I greatly revere grandfather's memory and firmly believe that 'friendly' quarrels are good for the health of large Protestant families like mine.

Born a small bundle of barely live flesh, Pili was immediately taken by my grandparents who, through numerous sleepless days and nights of loving care, saved his life. Grandfather had two cardinal rules in relation to his own male children, or to any other male child for that matter. A male child, as soon as he can stand, must not cry under any circumstance. A man, and all males of any age were men, must bear pain, sorrow, grief, anguish, without shedding tears or flinching. Secondly, a man must not be afraid of anything he can see, smell, touch, or of anything he thinks he can see, smell, hear, touch or taste. This included his own fears. And, above all else, a man must not be afraid of another man, or a group of men, or a gang of men, or an institution of men, or a government of men, or a mob of men. Any son of his had to have more courage than any other man, because of the fact that he was his son.

As soon as Pili could stand, grandfather took him everywhere he went, even to the meetings of the chiefs; carried him on his back, fed him, and when Pili wanted to urinate grandfather told him to do so right then and there and, whether it was in front of the other chiefs or the Governor or the Angels, grandfather didn't care and neither did Pili, later on. Pili slept beside him every night, shared his foodmat and conversation, listened to his vigorous repertoire of legends, yarns, platitudes, sermons, songs, speeches, prejudices, and to his extremely detailed knowledge of family, district and national history.

Pili, as soon as he started running and talking fluently, carried himself like grandfather: he'd enter any home in the village, without bowing his head, demand food, and get it because he was grandfather's son; he even began to verbally chastise adults and physically try to punish any child who offended him. When he could hold up his fists, grandfather trained him in the gentlemanly art of pugilism. And grandfather was a strict coach, no soft slaps, left or right hooks, but the fast-thrown clenched fist. Pili quickly learned to accept the punishment and also to dish it out.

The first real fight he had was with a boy twice his age and weight, and he came home crying. Grandfather ordered him to stop crying, like a man, and led him straight back to the other boy's home, like a man. They stopped on the road and grandfather, in his booming voice, ordered the other boy's father to send out his son. The father knew, as the other fathers knew, that he had to send out his son; if he didn't, grandfather would take him on. When the boy came out, grandfather said to Pili, 'Now I don't want to see you cry. If he hits you, beats you to mud, don't cry. Fight like a man!'

Pili was out-fought, out-fisted, out-everything from beginning to end, but he never fell down and he never cried;

43

he kept going in, face cut and bruised. Grandfather stopped the fight, took Pili home, washed his face, fed him, and analysed the mistakes he had made during the fight.

Early the next morning he led Pili back to confront the same opponent who, at this stage, was becoming an unwilling victor. (What do you do to a dwarf who refuses to give in? You hit him and hit him with everything you've got and he keeps coming back.) When they got there, the other boy's father came out and, stopping at a safe distance from grandfather, apologised aristocratically about his son's victory the day before. Grandfather accepted his apology aristocratically, but insisted on his son fighting Pili. Pili and the boy fought again. This time Pili made fewer mistakes. He lost the fight, but his opponent wasn't happy about his victory which had cost him a black-eye and a bloody nose. The next day, the third round of the marathon fight took place; it was a draw. In the fourth round, held the following morning, Pili had a slight edge. Before the fifth round, which took place on Sunday morning, the opponent's father cried as he pleaded with grandfather not to continue the fight. Fighting, he said, was extremely sinful and bad for young people. Has your son given in? grandfather demanded. Yes, yes! replied the father. Grandfather didn't believe him and the fight continued until, halfway through, Pili's opponent started bawling and saying please, please I don't want to fight anymore!

'There you are,' grandfather told a jubilant Pili as they walked home, 'victory is a matter of guts plus technique, but mainly guts. Fear is nothing. It's a matter of working at it. Chipping it away until you're scared no more and your guts are the guts of a man. Understand?' Pili nodded.

Similar fight marathons occurred during the following years. Pili always won, in the end. By the time Pili was about eleven, no young person in our village and district was willing to take him on. And from that time on, he stopped crying *genuine* tears. He didn't even cry when grandfather died. Grandmother will vouch for this.

Grandfather had a genuine respect for formal education, not that this urged him to insist on Pili attending the village school. You see, grandfather didn't have any respect whatsoever for the products of the education which he admired so much. He admired the process but not its products who, at this time, were mainly pastors and clerks whom grandfather called 'the primer six boys'. One of grandfather's favourite skits, which he performed when the 'primer six' were around, was to imitate a young pastor who had just graduated from Malua Theological College. He'd stand up in an imaginary pulpit, wearing an imaginary pair of lensless spectacles perched on the end of his nose, an imaginary starched white suit decked with pens, and an imaginary starched black tie, starched lavalava, shirt and sandals. Then, raising his eyebrows, arms outstretched as if he were getting ready to be crucified, he'd purse his lips, cough two short missionary coughs, and, in the bastardised Samoan used by papalagi missionaries, say: 'God . . . oh yes, God is not what we sinners think He is. Oh no yes. God is God. Amen'.

Grandfather certainly didn't want Pili to be a 'primer six boy' like his other sons. Pili went to the village school for a year, nearly made Miss Faafofoga have a nervous break-down, and, at the end of the year, refused to go again; grandfather agreed with him, and that was that. So while our family lived in the village Pili's education was limited to boxing, fishing, a bit of the pastor's school until Pastor Laau took to him with a thick guava branch and grandfather nearly took to Pastor Laau with his thick fists, oratory, Samoan history (or, more correctly, grandfather's biased version of it), plantation work once a week, and grandfather and more grandfather.

When Pili was about fifteen, my grandparents and Pili and most of my aunts shifted to Apia to the Vaipe, to live, and to enjoy my father's small plumbing business, a business which, before I was born, my father had established after he had finished his plumbing apprenticeship with an old German plumber. Grandfather had just turned sixty, but he looked twenty years younger. The main reason why he agreed to shift to town was this: the movement for self-government had erupted and Apia was alive and invigorat-ingly pregnant with forebodings of violent action and political intrigue, things so essential to grandfather's spiritual health. He also saw the movement as a god-given opportunity to prove once and for all to his enemies that he was a great orator and freedom fighter and nationalist leader.

According to grandmother, who is, I think, far less biased than the other members of my family, when grandfather and Pili hit the town they were like two children coming into possession of a new, marvellous, gorgeous but dangerous toy. Grandfather had visited Apia many times before, but somehow, with Pili at his side, the town took on a new meaning for him. Like a frisky fish taking to water, Pili took to the town. Like a barracuda turned saintly dolphin, grandfather took to the nationalist movement. And our family was, according to grandmother, never the same again: it became a family of both the town and the village, a family of two worlds *permanently*, and because of this, we were cursed by God with an arch-criminal, namely Pili. The curse is still with us to this day – ten months, one week and two days after Pili's death.

I have mentioned my grandmother many times already, yet I haven't discussed her role in Pili's life. She has denied any part of the blame. However, everyone knows that grand-mother, being grandmother, could not have helped but influence Pili. If grandmother had been capable of keeping a storm (namely grandfather) under control for over fifty years, I'm sure she had not been simply an innocent bystander in relation to Pili's upbringing. Beneath all her anger, criticism, disappointment with, and disavowals of Pili, I know that she loved him to the end. For can any genuine mother ever really deny a son even if he be a Devil, or a Barrabas, or a Cain?

She was born in Savaii, daughter of one of the first Samoan pastors, and spent her early childhood accompanying her parents over treacherous mountain passes, through dense bush, over white blazing beaches, and from island to island as they converted the people to Christianity, herself becoming one of the first Samoans to be able to read and write. At eighteen she attended Papauta Girls' College, a boarding school set up by the London Missionary Society to train young girls to become suitable wives for pastors; learned sewing, a few food recipes, reading and writing, a smattering of English and acquired a thorough knowledge of the Bible. Two years later, three weeks after meeting grandfather on a missionising excursion which the College had made to grandfather's village, she eloped with him. Her pastor father threatened to kill grandfather, so did her pastor mother, both of them putting the entire blame for the elopement on grandfather whom they referred to, from then on, as 'that pagan'. What grandmother never told them was that she had been entirely responsible for the elopement. Grandfather had wanted her to finish her last year at the College; however, she told him, in her usual hypnotising manner, that if he didn't come for her within three weeks she was never going to see him again, and that was that. Grandmother had heard a lot about grandfather's reputation. He was, at this time, notorious in our district for his escapades involving women, sometimes taking a wife for a few days and then sending her packing only to replace her with another one, touring the neighbouring villages either at night or on organised village trips, hunting female prey, brawling with any male who threatened to end his hectic love-life, threatening even our village pastor who had tried to verbally chastise him for his 'irresponsibility'.

A few weeks after eloping they got married in our village church, much to the astonishment and delight of the people in our district who had been expecting grandfather to ditch her. They saw her as a gentle, meek, almost inarticulate innocent young girl, exactly the picture she wanted them to have of her. This was the end of grandfather's notorious career as a lady-killer, as it were. He never looked at another woman again, or, let's say, that he might have looked but he never touched.

In public, grandmother never once revealed her power over grandfather. She, like Pili later on, was a 'smooth operator'. Grandfather died believing that he had been the absolute boss in the family, that all the major decisions regarding his family and village had been his. You see, unlike most modern women, grandmother knew that the secret to a man's heart was to make him believe all the time in his maleness, that he was sole ruler in his own house, and free, absolutely free to act as he pleased. Love was her means of controlling him, and I firmly believe that he loved her – something which is pretty rare in the marriages of their children and grandchildren. Grandfather's rages were well-known and feared. He'd break things (and people), yell, scream and perform, but to my knowledge he never once took his heavy hand to grandmother even though he was an outspoken advocater of wife-beating as a cure for spouse insolence and marital disagreements.

She had her way with the upbringing of their children, basing such upbringing on the cardinal virtues of puritanism: a good education the modern way, hard work, thrift, honesty, cleanliness, and godliness. The children all did well, becoming the best students at the pastor's school and, later on, the most conscientious students at the town schools, and uprighteous civil servants and pastors – apart from my father who became an uprighteous plumber. My father was the eldest, the one saddled by grandmother with the task of getting a job in order to pay for the education of the younger ones. Being the quietest and most dutiful of her sons, my father carried out her wish. And is now the wealthiest in the family and, even though still the quietest, he rules the family roost because, as he'll tell you in his rare moments of speech-making, usually when he's angry, the whole family owes him *everything*. None of his brothers and sisters, no matter how much more brilliant and educated they are than my father, can refute this because it's an irrefutable fact. The only one who could have refuted it, but never did, was Pili. Pili didn't owe my father his life, and I think this is one of the main reasons why my father never liked, trusted, or thought very much of him. You see, in order for my father to like you, you'll have to owe him just about everything you have, including the coffin you'll be buried in.

Grandmother adamantly maintains that grandfather, now long dead, should be held accountable for Pili's crimes. She argues that grandfather blamed her for the way the other children had turned out, and, in many ways, she agreed with him and admitted this by letting him take sole charge of Pili, their adopted son. However, knowing for a fact that she was the only other person that Pili admired and was afraid of, she must have influenced him in some major way. Ask yourself this question: why didn't Pili ever lie to grandmother when he lied to grandfather and everybody else when it suited him? I think, and this is the only sensible explanation which I've been able to come up with, that it was because of his fearful admiration for her. To discern her influence over Pili when he was a boy I've had to go on evidence provided by non-members of my family, especially on the evidence that grandfather's best friend, Taitolu Faavao, who is ninety-five and nearly toothlessly senile, has given me.

From the lengthy, sometimes terribly boring, rambling and disjointed conversations I've had with Taitolu, I can safely conclude, and I think this is the conclusion which any serious historian can draw from such evidence, that grandmother had a definite influence on Pili's mental and emotional development. Taitolu's evidence, to which I've had to apply the historical training which I was lucky to acquire at university in order to get at the facts buried in the rubble of Taitolu's wheezy, senile, romantic, hero-worshipping, mountainous memories, can be outlined thus:

The way Pili spoke, smiled and laughed when trying to con someone was the way grandmother spoke, smiled and laughed when controlling grandfather.

The way Pili was polite and almost invisible in public, yet you could always feel he was there, he copied from grandmother.

Pili's courage, which no one was able to break, was derived not only from grandfather but from grandmother. Grandfather took every opportunity to display his courage. On the other hand, grandmother did her best to keep hers hidden, just like Pili.

The way Pili charmed women was the way grandmother had charmed grandfather. The only difference was this: grandmother didn't use grandfather and then toss him out, whereas Pili used his women and when tired of them, departed.

Grandfather was blind to other people's hypocrisy and pretensions; grandmother wasn't, neither was Pili. Pili used people so effectively because, like grandmother, he knew their weaknesses so well.

Pili's absolute devotion to acting (and Pili played more convincing roles in his life than any other person I knew or know) was a reflection of grandmother's devotion to her role of controlling grandfather. Similarly, Pili's devout allegiance to a life of crime mirrored grandmother's allegiance to the church and the middle-way.

Grandmother's unshakable belief in godliness, thrift, hard work, cleanliness and honesty as the keys to a successful life was Pili's unshakable belief in ungodliness, spendthrift-ness, idleness, dirtiness and dishonesty as the ways to success.

In conclusion, you could almost say that grandmother and Pili had the same emotional and psychological makeup. Grandmother channelled hers towards what we call 'doing good', while Pili funnelled his into what we call 'doing wrong'.

But why had Pili been afraid of her? I think I know, now. Grandmother was the only person who knew him to the core of his being, who could see through all his numerous masks and touch him where he lived, inside; she was the only person who could have saved him from himself. But she loved him too much to act the role of saviour and redeemer, turn him into a saintly hero: she knew that he didn't want to be a hero because, to him, a hero was the supreme example of a confidence man, a charlatan, a spiritual thief, the hallowed devil on a white castrated charger or, in his own words: 'the heroes that people want are starch-suited merchants with expensive midget balls, peddling crippled nags'.

Grandfather and Son hit the town in the late 1920s, and grandfather became an outlaw member of an outlawed independence movement while his son quickly became an outlaw who specialised not in political subversion but in all forms of theft, graduating from stealing the neighbour's prize boar, giving cheek to the cops, conning unsuspecting children of their picture money and running a protection racket for all the youths of his age in the neighbourhood to burgling stores, houses and people that invited burgling. Grandfather found himself periodically in jail or detention camp or hiding in the bush because of his political activities; Pili began finding himself in jail, period.

In 1935, when the Labour Party came to power in New Zealand and gave political recognition to the Samoan Independence Movement, grandfather became a respectable political outlaw, while Pili continued to thrive in his life of crime. Grandfather never once condemned his son. Pili was no criminal, he'd tell my family – how could a son of his be an outlaw! The papalagi and half-caste cops were only picking on Pili because he was his son. He made this obviously clear to the Police by personally pulverising the Chief of Police and then promising to do the same to any other 'half-caste papalagi cop' who continued to pick on his son who was only a child. If you want to pick on anyone, he told the Police, pick on someone your age and size, like me for instance! Some misguided and jealous members of my family have tried to tell me that grandfather had been proud of Pili having been a criminal. Grandfather insisted that Pili was the only other *man* in his 'blasted' family, man and gutsy enough to take on anyone and anything.

After grandfather flattened their Chief, the Police always apologised to grandfather whenever they had to arrest Pili. Grandfather attended one of Pili's early trials but never went again after that. Grandmother heard about what grandfather had done at the Court, and she instructed him not to go again. In order not to lose face in front of his friends, grandfather informed them that he didn't like going to Pili's trials because he'd end up murdering that mockery of a papalagi judge. Pili had been charged with assault and battery, and to grandfather there was no such crime. Either one man beat up another man in a fair fight, and Pili always fought fairly, or he got beaten up. So that when Pili was fined, grandfather got up in the Court and challenged the Judge to a fair fight. The Judge refused and threatened him with a lengthy jail sentence if he didn't leave the Court-room at once. Grandfather picked up the bench he had been sitting on and instantly cleared the Court-room with it. Three Policemen had to hold him and force him out of the Court, with the Judge screaming legal epithets at him and grandfather shouting illegal epithets back. The terrified Policemen apologised to him as soon as the Judge was out of sight. My father, as always, paid Pili's fine and, as always, promised that he wasn't going to pay another penny for Pili's ungodly deeds. Grandfather, as always, calmed down and, by doing so, encouraged my extremely reluctant and thrifty father to continue paying Pili's fines later on.

The Second World War erupted, the American G.I. hordes came to Western Samoa, and Pili became the richest dollar criminal in the territory. You could almost say that the sex-hungry, grog-hungry G.I.s were made for Pili, and vice versa. Pili picked up G.I. English and dollars while the G.I.s picked up Pili's women (and the clap) and Pili's homebrew (and dysentery). Grandfather gained the most from Pili's new wealth. New clothes, cigars, shoes, suits, unlimited pocket money and a smattering of Pili's G.I. English. From 1940 to 1946, Pili didn't live at home, much to the relief of my family.

Pili, I forgot to mention, was a fanatical movie fan, and from gangster films he picked up new and more effective ways of improving his station in life. Organisation methods, for instance. Before the G.I.s arrived, my neighbourhood the Vaipe was famous for sly-grogging and part-time prostitution. However, none of the sly-grogging and girls were organised. To cater for the G.I. numbers, Pili organised the neighbourhood, put all the girls and grog under his control. Pili didn't use muscle (I think that's the word) to do it. He used clean business tactics and dazzling verbal persuasion. (Some of the friends he made, during what Pili called the 'Dollar Era', have told me that Pili was the only person they knew who could have talked 'the pants off an angel' or the Devil into becoming God.) If all the brews were put together and the methods of production improved, it'd mean bigger profits for all shareholders, he argued. Instead of every girl giving away her valuable wares for pennies, and doing her own soliciting, he argued that bigger money for all could be made if the girls formed a union which was managed by professionals like himself. A union would keep the prices up. 'Time saved means money made', was a phrase which he made popular during this period. In a short time the neighbourhood in which we lived, but were not a part of because of the high fence of moral purity around our acre of land, started swinging, hooked on the G.I. dollar and Pili's midas touch.

Pili never saved money. He spent it as fast as he got it, almost as if money was a fatal disease which, if kept too long in your pocket, would eventually kill you. So that when the G.I.s left at the end of the war, Pili was as broke as he had always been, and he returned to live at home, from whence he took enforced vacations to Tafaigata Prison, until grandfather died and my father, encouraged by the rest of the family, kicked him out for good. He went but he might as well have stayed because his record and crimes continued to haunt my uncles and aunts. Women, clutching newborn babies, would arrive at our home, looking for Pili or asking that our family should look after their babies. At the beginning, grandmother accepted all the children, and my parents had to care for them, reluctantly. But after the fifth time my father put his foot down. No more products of Pili's crimes, he told grandmother. 'No more! Haven't we ... haven't I paid enough for Pili's sins?' he yelled. 'From the day he was born, this family, and especially me, began paying, paying, paying!' Grandmother sought refuge in tears.

Not only did my family pay financially for their guilt regarding Pili, they also paid emotionally. It reached the stage where every time (which was often) someone mentioned that Pili was 'at it again' (a phrase which even strangers used when talking about Pili's latest crime), my father would get hysterically angry; Uncle Solomona would preach a homely sermon about the sins of parents becoming the bitter heritage of their children; Aunt Alofa would pray in her room; Aunt Ita would call for a thunderbolt to strike Pili dead; Aunt Fatu would gnash her false teeth and accuse whoever had told her of Pili's latest crime of being a vicious gossip; and grandmother would cry and say, 'I told him (grandfather). I told him. It was *all* his fault!'

As children we too had to live with Pili's now nationally-

known reputation, but, being children, my brothers and I
bragged about Pili to our friends. He was to us a fabulous
criminal like Robin Hood or Billy the Kid. I mean, what
other children in Samoa had an uncle who was, according
to everyone, the best criminal Samoa has ever produced.
Samoa had produced martyrs, clerks, politicians, murderers,
an occasional saint and a few civil servant intellectuals, but
never a criminal like Pili. When I was an adolescent,
interested in sex and sex, my admiration shifted to Pili's
career as a lady's man. What was Pili's secret, I wondered?
I mean, just look at him, a dwarf yet he gets all the women.
Me, I'm not bad looking yet no woman was interested. I
won a Government scholarship and left for New Zealand
believing, like every other middle-class, Protestant, well-
brought-up adolescent, that Pili's secret lay in the size of
his weapon, as it were. I hadn't actually seen it, but some of
my friends told me it was really 'something'.

I returned to Samoa every third Christmas, and every
time I came back Pili materialised out of the streets of Apia
to greet me, his 'intellectual nephew' who was an easy touch
for money, cigarettes, and new clothes. Right to his death,
I don't think he ever changed his opinion of me. He knew
that under all my formidable certificates and, later on, under
my M.A. degree, I was still an easy touch, or, in other
words, a fool. Quite frankly I didn't mind this. After all, the
substantial pocket money I had during my Christmas
vacations came from my father, and, as you already know,
my father had always paid for Pili's sins. Being the favourite
and most respected son in the family, I was being groomed
by Pili to replace my father as head of the family and
thereby become, like my father, a major source of easy
revenue. Pili forgot two things in his planning, though.
Firstly, he didn't know, and how was he to know, that he
was going to die before my father. Secondly, he didn't allow
for the fact that I was going to acquire a formidable wife
who was not going to let anyone else, except herself, spend
my hard-earned money. (I think Pili always believed that
I was incapable of getting a wife.)

Every Christmas when I met him we'd go to the pictures,
play billiards, go on sight-seeing tours round the island,

gorge ourselves on expensive food, and buy new clothes. Needless to say, I paid for everything with my father's money. Pili repaid me, without knowing it, with his superb acting, his marvellous yarns, his knowledge of the past of my family and his own unique views on life, race-horses, policemen, pastors, virgins, married women, politics and politicians, God, interplanetary travel, heroes and villains, and grandfather. To him, pastors were 'good but dangerous people'; 'virgins were to be "devirginised" because that's why virgins are virgins'; married women were not married women because women were by nature adulterous; politics were for politicians who were 'crooked but harmless sods'; God was God and he believed in God; interplanetary travel was a 'wicked and arrogant thing because where are the angels going to live?'; heroes were confidence men and villains were misunderstood men, and grandfather was a great memory he was completely unworthy of. Concerning women, Pili's secret was very simple. Here it is in his own words. You are free to follow his instructions if you have the courage; I never did.

'Tell them you love them, the fools. They're so gullible, they'll swallow your lies and all if you tell them you love them. See what I mean? Get them to bed fast and give them a galloping orgasm. Then tell them they're a dead loss in bed. Get what I mean? Then ditch them and they'll come after you like randy race horses to try and prove they're not dead losses. Bash them up a few times. I mean, all women like to be handled like you're God or something. They like to feel you don't need them. Get me, uh? But you've got to be awake all the time. When you feel they're getting their claws into you, ditch them for good. Remember you're only doing them a favour, ditching them for their own good, not yours. They love being kicked out. I mean that gives them an excuse to take on another man. You're educated enough to know that if someone likes something so much, you're only doing them a good turn by doing what they want. Get me?'

Similarly, all people like being fleeced of their money, property, souls, honesty, religion, purity and innocence – according to Pili. 'All these things are problems to them, and who wants problems! Why do you think people created the Devil, uh? You answer me that. I mean you've got education, you read and write better than all the natives here. Why do you think we created the Devil? We made him up so that he can take away our problems. See?'

'Is that why they call you "the pint-size devil on a thoroughbred"?' I asked him.

He blinked, and gazing at me as if I was the Devil, asked, 'Is that what they call me?' I nodded, trying to keep a straight face. 'But . . . but I'm no devil. I mean, I don't fleece people of their *problems*!' he declared.

Right to the day he died, he never admitted to me that he was a confidence man, a thief, a liar, a crook, and a gangster. I don't think he ever admitted it to himself either. He was like an alcoholic who firmly believes that he isn't an alcoholic, that's one interpretation which cured alcoholics or liberals would offer you. Another explanation might be that, like grandfather, he believed that he wasn't doing anything wrong if he believed he wasn't doing anything wrong. That doesn't mean that Pili thought that there was no such thing as a crime or a sin. For example, he believed that murder, beating children, poisoning fish and animals and people, abortion, encouraging people not to part with their *problems* (namely, their money, property, goods, and anything else they considered were problems), were wrong, sinful, and against the law – his law.

After spending what seemed a lifetime conning my way through a degree – something which, if I had told Pili, would have made him change his low opinion of me – I returned to Samoa, with a wife who soon after caused Pili's low opinion of me to deteriorate further. Because my wife couldn't be 'fleeced of her problems' Pili's visits to our house decreased, drastically. Whenever he was out of jail or in Apia he took to ringing me up to come and meet him in town. I went whenever I could, without my wife knowing.

A year before he served his last jail sentence, while he was in jail for a month for assault and battery, the Police

Department introduced one major prison reform: model prisoners were to be allowed to visit their families every week-end. Pili immediately became a model prisoner, got word to his last wife that she and her child were still his family so that the cops could be persuaded that he had a 'lovely wife and child' to visit, and was allowed out in the week-ends. He never once visited that poor woman and her child. He stayed with us the first week-end he came out, much to my wife's regret and to mine because it was the first time I nearly assaulted my wife – for not making Pili's visit a pleasant one. During the second week-end he stayed with Uncle Solomona who had recently been appointed pastor to our village on the other side of the island. When Pili returned to prison on Monday morning Uncle Solomona came to Apia and for two hours, while my grandmother and aunts cried, Solomona outlined, in language very similar to Pili's usual spiel, how he (Solomona, a 'humble pastor') had re-converted Pili to our church. Even my wife began to change her views about her Uncle Pili. My father sat with bowed head. I got up, went outside, and laughed. Pili's conversion was merely Pili proving he could con Solomona whom he referred to as 'an amateur con-man'. I was absolutely correct. Solomona returned to our village to find two extremely angry parents who accused him of having given sanctuary to a devil who had seduced their innocent daughters. Solomona also discovered that his three best sports-shirts and a pair of sandals were missing. Also, the £8 from the previous Sunday's church collection. He didn't want our family to laugh at him so he didn't go to the Police, just as Pili had planned. You see, Pili believed that the main weakness of 'amateurs' was their boastful pride. A professional never boasted about his success because he didn't have an ounce of pride in his veins. Pili didn't have a face to lose, whereas Solomona had an over-sized one to be laughed at, as it were. This, according to Pili, was the only difference between a pastor such as Solomona, and a lay man like himself.

When he was finally released from prison, he disappeared into Savaii for a few months. We heard a lot about him, and what we heard were the usual things we had heard about him ever since he was born. As he drifted back closer and closer to town, from the outer reaches of Savaii, the usual became more usual and more nerve-racking for the elders in my Protestant family who had prayed that he'd stay in the outer, more uncivilised regions of the big island. An irate parent here and there, a pregnant woman there and there, a divorce here, a fleeced planter or merchant there, rumours of a vendetta here, men without matai titles (which they had paid Pili for) there, a converted or stolen truck here, and a jilted wife at the last village he was at. It was the usual geographical map which Pili drew up whenever he decided to roam a whole island, relieving people of their problems and acquiring a few more facial scars.

Until, looking chubby and fit on other people's problems, he appeared at my house wherein, for about a week, I had to live with an almost hysterical wife and a smiling, charming, from-dawn-till-sunset-talking, uninvited guest who liked steak and eggs for breakfast, lunch and tea; ready-made American cigarettes in chains; hot showers morning, noon and night; browsing through my collection of books and magazines which he couldn't read, and leaving it all over the floor for my wife and the house-girl to put back into place; calling my razor, clothes, shoes, and everything else, *ours*; teaching my already spoilt two-year-old daughter to swear at her parents, grandparents, grand-uncles and great grandmother, in Samoan and G.I. English; encouraging me to rebel against my own kinfolk who, he maintained, were kinfolk he loved, respected and admired; pestering my house-girl with ogling proposals of marriage and children (him not being the man everyone had told her he was); cutting the papalagi neighbours' lawns at ten shillings an hour and yet never offering to cut *our* lawn; getting me, the historian in the family, to write down our family history and lineage which, he said, was blue-blooded aristocracy; offering me the highest titles in our family which, according to him, grandfather had bestowed upon him and over which he therefore had sole control and would bestow upon me if I wanted them. After his first day with us my wife could have murdered him, my house-girl thought he was pleasantly insane, my daughter thought he was God, my dog growled

58

and slunk away whenever he was around, and I, even though my ulcer began playing up again and my hard-earned money as a teacher began disappearing fast, became convinced that he was extremely convivial, stimulating, intellectual company, far more so than the rest of my god-fearing, dull family. But I knew he had to leave – because of my wife, my house-girl, my dog, my ulcer, and my money. He knew this, but instead of leaving without telling anyone he asked me for money to buy books for his children. He didn't want to act out of character because he knew that I admired his role as the devil on a thoroughbred. He wanted, in other words, to repay me for my hospitality. I acted my expected role as an easy touch in order not to disillusion him; I gave him a pound, and he departed in a taxi which he got my wife to ring for.

If I had known what was going to happen I would not have given him that money. That pound bought him his last jail sentence which cost him his life. I betrayed him with money, the disease which he always gave away as soon as he had fleeced it off someone else. Those twenty pieces of silver cost me the only man I ever admired and respected in my family.

Pili died trying to save a couple of Police wardens who were drowning in the river which flows through the Tafaigata Prison plantation. Incredible, isn't it? But every eye-witness to the event will bear witness to Pili's heroism. He saved one warden, and drowned trying to save another. Both cops were the most sadistic in the Force, according to most of the prisoners who served time with Pili and to the few cops I know well. Why Pili bothered to rescue them they'll never know. But even if we'll never understand his motives for doing it, by trying to save sadism (evil), as it were, he became a national hero, our type of hero. His act was worthy of a Victoria Cross and a Knighthood (speaking figuratively now because Samoa can't make these awards), an act worthy of admission into Paradise – and Samoa, being Christian, can award such a passport. Pili, by rescuing evil from the clutches of the raging river (Nature), turned all the 'evil deeds' he had committed while on earth into beautiful and heroic ballads which you'll hear adults and children sing and tell today. I suppose if Hitler had, at the last minute, repented for the evil he had done we would have forgiven him, have composed ballads about him being a knight combating evil Jews, rescuing Christians from the clutches of Einsteins and Dayans – just as our human predecessors created heroes out of unshaven, psychopathic, cold-blooded murderers like Robin Hood, Billy the Kid, Al Capone, Jack the Ripper, and Bluebeard.

Here is a ballad which some truly creative balladeer has composed about Pili.

### Ballad of Pili the Kid

The storm broke, and the river raged
while young Pili slaved
to cut the gov'ment's timber.
Tafaigata Prison was a hellish hell
for our young courageous Pili,
a stone cold hell for Pili.


Two evil wardens, Mike and Mick, watched
while Pili and his chained compan's slaved
to cut the gov'ment's timber.
Not a pause to rest, no food to eat
to relieve their agonee,
no God to set them free.


In the cold, cold storm they worked
making money for our fair countree.
One of Pili's friends, oldman John,
collapsed to knee in frightful agonee,
Mike and Mick, both heartless men, whipped
oldman John to his shaking feet.


'I'll kill you, John,' Mike he did scream
'We'll kill any man who stops,' said Mick.
And brave Pili and his ten compan's
slaved on, slaved on in agonee.
'Is there no mercy in our police?'
thought Pili pitifully.

60

The thunder cracked mightily,
the lightning flashed and screamed,
and not a rest had they
until oldman John collapsed
and died of a stroke he did.
O God, may Your bright light shine on him.


Mike and Mick in their cruelty
picked up brave John's cadavie
and into the raging stream
they hurled it in, it in.
O God in Heav'n have mercy on him,
forgive brave John the Pimp.


Our brave young Pili worked on,
but his ten compan's in chains
turned on heartless Mike and Mick,
they could stand no more agonee
and they pushed the ward'ns into the stream,
and deserved it well they did.


Brave young Pili broke off his chains
and jumped into the stream.
Watch him against the tide to swim
to rescue the warden Mike drowning,
he brings him safely to the bank
and goes to rescue Mick.


The raging river envelops him
and no more do we see
our brave young Pili so free,
so just as ev'ry man should be.
But don't you weep, my fair countree,
'Cause our Pili is in Heav'n, he is.


So all who are listening to me,
my sad sad tale is free,
don't forget brave Pili the Kid
and his rescue of evil in the stream.
Model your life, your ev'rything
on our brave Pili the Kid.

The above ballad is, at the moment, very popular in my country. The English translation is mine; the ballad, I'm sorry to say, is not mine. My father, through some of his politician friends, has tried and is still trying to have it banned from our local radio station. His reasons for trying are not my reasons for hoping that the ballad is banned. I object to the ballad in its present form, it contains many major errors. My father, aunts and uncles find the ballad highly objectionable because, everytime it is played over the air, Pili, and a heroic Pili at that, returns to haunt them.

In my view the spirit of the ballad is absolutely correct, proper and appropriate. However, some of the events and details as described by the balladeer, who obviously didn't do much research before composing his ballad, are incorrect. I've been trying, ever since the ballad came out on the air, to trace the composer in order to congratulate him on his masterly composition and point out some of the grave errors in it.

For instance, Pili was fifty-five when he died – he was far from being 'our young Pili'. Tafaigata Prison, as it was when Pili was there last year, was not a 'hellish hell' or a 'stone cold hell'. Overseas visitors, some of them specialising in visiting prisons wherever they travel, have described Tafaigata in the press as being 'very modern and comfortable'. The reference made by the composer to the prisoners having worn chains is absolutely incorrect. I have been told by the Commissioner of Police and certain trustworthy ex-convicts that chains went out at the beginning of this century. Another major error is the reference to 'oldman John'. As far as I've been able to find out, John the Pimp was only thirty when he died. Again, in relation to John, the composer is misguided in pleading a strong case for John having been a good, peace-loving man. John the Pimp was a liar, a thief, and a male prostitute; he was only a pimp part-time. His 'cadavie' was later found, and in an autopsy it was discovered that he had been dying from some rare kidney disease caused by too much drinking. John didn't die from a stroke. Some of Pili's ten 'compan's' mentioned in the ballad have told me that Mike didn't say to John, 'I'll kill you, John'. What he said was, 'Look,

John, stop pretending you're sick'. And what Mick said was, 'Your week-end leave will be cancelled if you don't work harder', not, 'We'll kill any man who stops'. By the way, the real names of the wardens were not Mike and Mick. The one whom Pili rescued was, and still is, called Manupé. He was recently made a sergeant. The one who drowned was called Solofanua. His wife has since married another Policeman, a sub-inspector. But I can understand the composer's motives behind giving them false names. Libel and slander is an expensive business. It is grossly misleading of the composer to claim that Pili thought, 'Is there no mercy in our police?' He couldn't have thought that because Pili *knew*, was absolutely convinced, that our police had no mercy.

The composer's astounding claim that Pili is in 'Heav'n' is to my way of thinking, a false assumption. There is no such place; and even if there was (or is) Pili told me, for a fact, that he never wanted to go there. The inference, contained in the second to last verse, that Pili's body wasn't found again is absolutely untrue. It was found a few miles downstream two days later. All the ribs were smashed, the face dented in, and his brain, an organ which my family had always claimed didn't exist in Pili's head, had broken open.

It is a sad pity that the ballad ends without describing, or at least saying, where Pili was buried and why he was buried there. You see, the balladeer's hero was buried in jail in an unmarked grave because my family wanted it that way. His epitaph can be easily constructed from the statements uttered by his brothers and sisters (and my wife) when they heard that Pili was dead:

*Aunt Fatu*: 'He deserved it.'

*Aunt Alofa*: 'What did you expect from the son of a Chinaman.'

*Aunt Ita*: 'Why did he have to go and be a hero? Now he's going to ruin everything.'

*Uncle Solomona*: 'Let us pray for his salvation.'

*My father*: 'I knew he'd die someday.'

*My wife*: 'Poor man, poor man.'

My grandmother wept as she had wept when grandfather died. Me? I got drunk for the first time in my life, not because I wanted to get drunk but because Pili would have wanted me to celebrate his final victory, over our family, with vodka, whisky, bacardi, rum and all the other drinks he loved so much.

It is nearly a year now since Pili died, and most of my family are still trying to convince themselves that Pili betrayed them by dying a hero's death; they want to believe that he should have died as the devil; as one of the damned; as the soulless unremitting sinner he had been all his life; as the curse God had sent to punish them. Perhaps Pili chose to become their kind of hero in order to haunt them from the grave. I don't know. Perhaps he did it as a practical joke on all the people who believed he was a devil. Perhaps he did it in order to be worthy of grandmother's love. At times I want to believe that he did it so that I'd change what he thought was my opinion of him. Perhaps he did it so that a God of Love, in Whom he didn't believe, could be believed in. Perhaps he did it to prove to every criminal that they too could, through one heroic act, become national heroes. Perhaps he chose to die violently because grandfather had died of an ulcer and in bed. And then again, the way he died could have been an *accident*, the one time in his life when faced with an emergency, he acted out of character without realising it and, as he had always feared, paid for it with his life. In the final instance – and this is a view which is totally unacceptable to the rest of my family apart from my grandmother – in dying as our type of hero he betrayed himself, betrayed his life-long belief that heroes, our heroes, are 'starched-suited merchants with expensive midget balls, peddling crippled nags'.

During the last few weeks as I tried to write this, to resurrect him from the vault of memory, I have heard him chuckling in the wind and rain buffeting the house, chuckling at my thoughts of him, as though saying, 'You, nephew, will never succeed in pinning me to paper. The one you've got down is only a pampered nag with golden overweight teeth.'

# A Resurrection

Tala Faasolopito died at 2.30 p.m. yesterday at Motootua Hospital: we heard about it over the radio. He died, so the doctors have diagnosed, of coronary thrombosis. He also died one of the most respected and saintly pastors of the Congregational Church (and of the whole nation therefore).

He was born in the Vaipe, oldest son of Miti and Salamo Faasolopito, both now deceased, and a brother to three sisters and two brothers, whose names I've forgotten. However, the Vaipe has not seen Tala for over forty years, ever since he walked out of it in 1920, at the age of nineteen. I never knew him. What I know about him I have gained from my father and other Vaipe people who knew him. Or, let me say, the Tala I know is a resurrection, a Lazarus resurrected from the memory-bank of the Vaipe.

Tala did not kill the man who had raped his sister, he walked out of the Vaipe and into Malua Theological College to become an exemplary man of God. He never again set foot in the Vaipe. Not even when his father deserted his mother, not even when his mother died of a broken heart (so my mother has concluded) four years later, not even when his brothers and sisters disappeared one by one from the Vaipe in an attempt to escape his (Tala's) disgrace which had become *their* disgrace. The Vaipe was his cross, and he never wanted to confront it again. I once read an article about him in the 'Bulletin', 12th September, 1959: his place of birth, the Vaipe, was never once mentioned in that article. Tala became, for most of our extremely religiously-minded countrymen, a symbol of peace and goodwill, a shining example of virtuous, civilised and saintly living. But to most Vaipe people he was still Tala, the nineteen-year-old who had refused to become a man, their type of man sprung free like elephant grass from fertile Vaipe mud. Not that they did not become proud of him when he became a 'saint' (my father's description). They forgave him. But I believe that Tala never forgave himself. His choice not to avenge his sister's (family) honour determined the course of his life, the very sainthood he grew into. And he regretted that choice.

I possess copies of three of his now nationally-quoted sermons. The sermons are not very original; they reveal little of their composer or the heart of the religion he believed in; they are the usual-type sermons you hear over 2AP every Sunday night without fail. However, I also have the originals of two sermons which he composed a few months before he died and which he never made public. (My father, who grew up with Tala, got the originals from Tala's wife, Siamomua.)

The first sermon, dated Monday, 27th October, 1968, and written in an elaborate and ornate longhand (Tala went to Marist Brothers' School famous for such handwriting) on fragile letter-writing paper, is entitled: 'A Resurrection of Judas'. The second sermon, a typewritten script forty pages in length, is more a private confession than a sermon. It is dated 25th December, 1968, and under the date is this title printed in pencil: 'On the Birthday of Man'. A public perusal of these two sermons would have reduced Tala, in the fickle minds of the public, from saint to madman. For instance, in 'A Resurrection of Judas', Tala offers us a compellingly original but disturbing conclusion: 'Judas Iscariot was the Christ. He did not betray Jesus. Jesus betrayed Judas by not stopping him from fulfilling the prophecy.'

I think that the key to the door into the endless corridors that were Tala's life was his choice not to avenge his family's honour.

As a child I used to play under the breadfruit trees surrounding the fale which belonged to Tala's family; this was after Tala had left the Vaipe for good. Tala's mother, who was a big woman with five chins (or so it seemed then) and long black hair streaked with grey, and an uncontrollable cough (they said she had Tb), and ragged dresses that hung down her like animal skins, sometimes invited me into the main fale to play with her children. They were much older than me but they condescended to play hopscotch, sweepy, and skipping with me. I sometimes ate with them, mainly boiled bananas and sparse helpings of tinned herrings. (They were poor, so my parents told me.) I really enjoyed those times. The fale and shacks are still there today, reminding me, every time I pass them, of a contented childhood, but the people (distant relatives of the Faasolopitos) who now occupy them are strangers to me.

I often ran over the muddy track, leading over the left bank of the Vaipe from the ageless breadfruit trees, to the home of the family of the man, Fetu, who, by raping Tala's sister, became the springboard of Tala's life. The track is still there, like a string you can use to find your way out of a dense forest, but Fetu is dead, he has been dead for a long time – he died in prison, stabbed to death by another prisoner who could have been Tala twenty years before because Tala should have killed Fetu but didn't.

Tala and his ill-fated family, and Fetu, and this whole section of the Vaipe are anchored into my mind and made meaningful by the memory of that awesome deed which Tala did not commit; by the profound and unforgettable presence of the ritual murder which Tala and his family and most of the inhabitants of the Vaipe committed in their hearts, and which has become a vital strand of my heritage of memories – a truth which Tala, by avoiding it, had to live with all his life.

'We are what we remember: the actions we lived through or should have lived out and which we have chosen to remember.' Tala has written this in his sermon, 'On the Birthday of Man', page five.

Tala's ordeal, his first real confrontation with the choice that separates innocence from guilt, occurred the night of 3rd March, 1920.

Behind the Vaipe, stretching immediately behind Tala's home up to Togafuafua and Tufuiopa and covering an area of a few uninhabited square miles, is a swamp. An area, into which a number of fresh water springs find their way turning the soil into mud and ponds, alive with crabs and shrimps and watercress and waterlily and wild taro and taamu and tall elephant grass and the stench of decay and armies of mosquitoes. Scene of children's war games: cowboys and Indians, massacres and ambushes and mudfights. Tala, so my father has told me, was the most skilful and adept crab and shrimp hunter in the Vaipe. His father (still remembered and referred to in the Vaipe as 'that spineless, worthless failure') was incapable of supporting his large family. He despised work of any type or form. So the burden of feeding and clothing and keeping the family together was left to Miti and Tala. She worked as a house-servant for expatriates, while Tala, who had left school at standard four, stayed home during the day to care for the younger children, and to forage for food. The swamp became a valuable source of food: succulent crabs and shrimp, taro and taamu. Sometimes he sold these at the market to get money to buy other essentials, such as kerosene for the lamp, matches, sugar, salt and flour.

The children always looked clean and healthy and happy, so I've been told. (When I came on the scene five years after Tala's departure, the Faasolopito children I played with were dirty, unkempt and spotted with yaws.) 'There was enough love and laughter and food to go around then', my father tells me. The eldest girl (and her name is of no importance to this story), a year younger than Tala, was extremely beautiful: a picture of Innocent Goodness, some Vaipe elders have described her to me.

The youth who emerged from the swamp that evening as the cicadas woke in a loud choral chant was on his way to meet a saint, a destiny he wasn't aware of yet. He was tired and covered with mud after a whole afternoon of digging for crabs; but now the thought of a cool shower and a hot meal and the smell and warmth of his family was easing his aching, as he went through the tangled bamboo grove on to the track that led to his home ahead – behind clumps of banana trees he had planted the Christmas before. Something brushed against his forehead, a butterfly? He looked

up and saw through the murmuring bamboo heads a sky
tinted with faint traces of red; the sun was setting quickly.
Tomorrow there would be rain. As he moved past the banana
trees the broad leaves caressed his arms and shoulders like
the cool feathery flow of spring water. He saw the fale, oval
and timeless in the fading light. (He took no notice of the
group of people in the fale.) He veered off towards the
kitchen fale expecting, at any moment, his youngest brother
to come bursting out of the fale to greet him and inspect
his catch. But no one came. He looked at the main fale
again, at the silent group gathered like a frightened brood
of chickens round the flickering lamp. Knew that something
was terribly amiss. He dropped the basket of crabs and ran
towards the light; towards the future he would avoid – to
attain a sainthood that he would, on confronting the
reality of old age, deny – in order to *be* Judas.

Tala walked – more a shuffle than a walk – towards Fetu's
fale, trying to overcome the feeling of nausea which had
welled up inside him the moment he had pulled the bushknife
out of the thatching of the kitchen fale. The bushknife, now
clutched firmly in his right hand, was a live, throbbing
extension of his humiliation and anger and doubts and fear
of the living deed which he had to fulfil in order to break
into the strange, grey world of men. His whole life was now
condensed into that cross-shaped piece of violent steel,
a justification for Fetu's murder; 'my murder', Tala has
written in 'On the Birthday of Man'. Fetu's imaginary
murder was also his own murder, Tala believed. 'There is
no difference between an *imagined* act and one actually
committed'.

He stopped in the darkness under the talie trees in front
of Fetu's house – a small shack made of rusting corrugated
iron and sacking. The clinking of bottles and glasses and
the sound of laughter were coming from the shack. (Fetu
operated what is known in the Vaipe as a 'home-brew den';
he had already served two prison terms for the illegal
brewing of beer.) Tala had never been in the shack before,
even when he had been sent by his mother to fetch his
father, who sometimes came to Fetu's den to get violently

drunk. He knew Fetu quite well, as well as he knew most of the other men in the Vaipe. He went up the three shaky steps and into the shack.

At the far corner, under the window and partly covered by shadow, squatted an old man, still as an object. In the middle of the room three youths were drinking at the only table. He knew them and they knew him, but they said nothing, they just stopped drinking and watched him. Tala saw no one else in the room. He went up and stopped in front of the three youths. The mud had dried on his skin and it felt like a layer of bandages throughout which blood had congealed. All the walls of the room were covered with pictures clipped randomly from newspapers and magazines, and the one light-bulb that dangled from the middle rafter gave the pictures a dream-like quality, ominous and unreal. A few empty beer bottles lay scattered across the floor, glistening in the harsh light.

'Are you looking for him?' one of the youths asked. Tala nodded. (Fetu and his family lived in the back room, but no sound came from that room.)

'He isn't here,' the same youth said.

'I . . . have . . . I have to,' but he couldn't say it; it was too difficult and final a step to take into the unknown.

'To *kill* him?'

'Yes,' he said.

'Yes, you *have* to kill him,' the other two youths said. It was as if the youths (and the Vaipe) had resolved that he should kill Fetu, or die trying.

Tala turned slowly and left the shack. He told himself that he wasn't frightened.

No one in the Vaipe knows what happened next, for there was no one there to observe what Tala did before leaving the Vaipe forever. To the rich-blooded inhabitants of the Vaipe, a tale without an exciting (preferably violent) climax, no matter how exaggerated and untrue that climax may be, is definitely *not* a tale worth listening to. A yarn or anecdote especially concerning courage, must, in the telling, assume the fabulous depths and epic grandeur of true myth. And, being a Vaipean to the quick of my honest fingernails, I too cannot stop where actual fact ends and conjecture (imagination) begins; where a mortal turns into maggot-meat and the gods extend into eternity, as it were. So for Tala's life, for my Lazarus resurrected, let me provide you with a climax.

Tala waited under the talie trees until the youths had left the shack and the light had been switched off; until he glimpsed someone (Fetu?) slipping into the back room of the shack; until he thought that Fetu had fallen asleep; then, without hope (but also without fear), he groped his way round the shack to the back room and up into the room which stank of sweat and stale food.

A lamp, turned quite low, cast a dim light over everything. Two children lay near the lamp, clutching filthy sleeping sheets round their bodies. On the bed snored Fetu; beyond him slept his wife. Tala moved to the bed and stood above Fetu. He raised the bushknife. He stopped, the bushknife poised like a crucifix above his head. Mosquitoes stung at the silence with their incessant drone.

'Forgive me,' he said to the figure on the bed which, in the gloom, looked like an altar. Carefully, he placed the bushknife across Fetu's paunch, turned, recrossed the threshold and went out into the night and towards an unwanted sainthood in our scheme of things.

In 'On the Birthday of Man', page forty, second to last paragraph, Tala writes: 'I believe now that to have killed then would have been a liberation, my joyous liberation.'

My father, a prominent deacon in the Apia Congregational Church, is getting dressed to go to Tala's funeral service. (Tala's wife wants him to be one of the pallbearers.)

I'm not going to the funeral.

It is only a saint they are burying.

# The Coming of the Whiteman

Many sons and daughters of the Vaipe have gone to New Zealand to live and work. Most of them are still there. A few have returned once or twice to bury their parents and have then flown back never to be heard from again. One of the first to return to stay permanently was Peilua, son of Alapati who was one of the most respected men in the Vaipe: most respected because he had a highly-envied job as a pharmacist in the Motootua Hospital Dispensary; most respected because he belonged to the so-called 'educated elite' of the Vaipe (and that elite numbered only four or five during Alapati's lifetime); most respected because, even though he never went to church, he still loved his neighbours and helped any of them who needed help. When Alapati died, a few years back, his funeral was one of the most memorable events in Vaipe history. Most Vaipe people attended his funeral; so did Mr F.A. Jones – the head pharmacist at the Dispensary; so did Mr T.B. Muel – Assistant Director of Health; and so did many other notable personalities from all over Upolu and Savaii. In the Vaipe, a man's funeral can make or unmake the reputation that he leaves to posterity. 'It was a magnificent occasion; he went to God well-prepared and well-mourned', the old people would say after attending a particularly sumptuous funeral. Or, if the funeral was a miserly one, 'It was a shame his mean family had to farewell him *that* way'. No matter how poor you are, you must die and be buried in style, with lots of food and fine mats and solemn prayers and speeches, and in a concrete grave anchored down with a black marble tombstone. Alapati was buried in style and with style, befitting his elite status in the Vaipe. Now deaths and funerals of loved ones shouldn't really concern the able-bodied, frisky and optimistic young who, after all, have years and years to live out yet. But Alapati's funeral did concern Peilua, his youngest and most intelligent and favourite son whom Alapati sent to New Zealand to work during the day, attend night school, go on to pharmacy school and return to Samoa a brilliant pharmacist like Alapati himself. Peilua, the first year in Wellington, New Zealand, did attend work (as a wharfie) during his daylight hours; and he did diligently attend night school from 6.30 p.m. to 10.30 p.m. every weeknight; and he did conscientiously attend the Samoan Congregational Church in Newtown twice every Sunday; and he did write faithful letters to his family every week. That was in 1953. In 1954, however, he wrote only four letters: one during his New Year holidays; one during Easter – Black Friday to be exact; one during White Sunday; and one dated the 1st December 1954, four weeks before he reappeared in person in the Vaipe, carrying a massive and expensive suitcase. (That day will always be referred to in the Vaipe as 'The Day of the Coming of the Whiteman'.)

Alapati, through his second wife, Misa, who hadn't given birth to Peilua, disseminated the story that Peilua had returned because of ill-health – he had always been a delicate boy. But within a matter of two days everyone in the Vaipe knew that Peilua, Alapati's most favourite son, had been deported from New Zealand. Peilua himself was responsible for telling *that* truth. The second night he was back he got drunk with some of his friends at Fofoga's home-brew den, and confessed what he called 'the whole truth and nothing but the truth'. Well, it wasn't really a confession: he bragged about it. That same night, after his friends carried him home, Alapati nearly beat him to death. The next morning, Peilua, face swollen and cut and stitched, shifted out of his father's elaborate and spacious fale to live in his Uncle Tomasi's dingy home which was only three fale away. He took with him what the Vaipe people came to refer to as 'Peilua's wondrous suitcase'.

Alapati never again talked to Peilua directly, until the morning before he died. He summoned Peilua to his bedside. Peilua, always an optimist because that was the way his father had brought him up, went expecting Alapati to ask him for *his* forgiveness. What he got was a curse: 'I put a curse on you and on that woman you're living with and any illegitimate children you may have!' exclaimed Alapati. From that moment on Peilua ceased being an optimist. He became a haunted man; he had to carry his death – a father's irrevocable and final curse – with him wherever he went. This is what the Vaipe elders would tell you. For a man cursed by his mother or father (or grandmother or grandfather) is doomed like the Devil whom God cursed into Hell. What finally happened to Peilua was predetermined and made inevitable by his father's dying curse.

When Peilua was exiled from his father's house, he didn't worry over much about it. He didn't even bother to find work, or return and apologise to his father (as his father wanted and expected him to). Uncle Tomasi and his wife and their eight children shifted to live in the right-hand side of their fale while Peilua took occupation of the left-hand side, the only bed, the best sleeping mats, and the newest mosquito net.

He became a highly esteemed house-guest, treated by the Tomasis like an important papalagi visitor. He was fed the best food and given the best service by Tomasi who was proud to have him live there, because Peilua was 'so educated and so like a whiteman'. In fact, when conversing with other people, the Tomasi family began referring to Peilua, in all seriousness, as 'our relative, the papalagi'. To Tomasi, nothing was too good for his nephew whom his ungrateful brother Alapati did not deserve as a son.

The Tomasi family were the first fortunate mortals to glimpse the wonders of Peilua's suitcase.

Every early afternoon without fail, when Peilua decided to get out of bed, Tomasi's wife and children would gather in the fale and watch Peilua getting ready to go out. Whistling merrily, he would open the suitcase, get out his silver razor, red toothbrush and hand-mirror, and then leave to shower behind the fale. The children would follow him.

Never before had they seen such a razor and mirror. Mrs Tomasi would watch from the fale. Peilua usually took an hour shaving and showering. Then one of the children would hand him one of his elaborately designed towels and he would dry himself delicately just like the film stars the children had seen in American movies.

Back in the fale, he would open two bottles of perfume (they could give it no other name but this), pour some of the dazzling lotion into his hands and pat it into his face. Mrs Tomasi, who sometimes took illegal peeps into Peilua's suitcase without his permission, would hand him his sleek black comb and, after rubbing hair-oil – a liquid kind never before seen in the Vaipe – into his black wavy hair, Peilua would slide the comb through it in long delicate strokes while one of the children, chosen by Peilua on standards of hygiene and cleanliness, held up the hand-mirror for him. After this wonderful ritual, they would watch him open his suitcase and, taking out his almost unlimited supply of sports-shirts, select one, unfold it and put it on carefully. (The colours and designs of his shirts outranged a bright rainbow, and only Mrs Tomasi was allowed to wash and iron them.) Out of the fabulous depths of the suitcase would then come a pair of trousers, selected after a lengthy period of considering the weather and the purpose of his outing and the condition of Vaipe soil surface. Peilua would disappear behind the curtain which separated his bed from the more mundane world of the rest of the fale and, after the sound of more happy whistling, he would emerge smiling; and the family would sigh, and almost cheer and clap, at the sight of legs and buttocks sheathed in expensive, permanently-pressed, perfectly-tapered trousers, at the sight of feet shod in silk socks. (Peilua, so Mrs Tomasi told her husband in hushed tones late one night, had fifteen pairs of these marvellous trousers. He even gave Tomasi a pair of ragged, faded jeans the week after he shifted in: they were Tomasi's prized possession which he wore only once a month – when he went to collect his pay from the office of the company where he worked as night watchman.) Mrs Tomasi would then slip courteously past Peilua and bring out, from under his bed, his eight pairs of shoes, which she would line up before him like an army of polished soldiers. He would scrutinise the shoes and point at a pair and at one of the children. The child would rush forward with a rag, polish the shoes in record time, and raise them up to Peilua. Smiling, Peilua would then put them on. Another child, whom Peilua had spent one week teaching how to properly lace and tie shoes, would scramble forward on his knees and tie the shoes. Peilua would then take out two silk handkerchiefs, sheathe one in his shirt pocket and one in his trouser pocket. The golden wrist-watch would then come out of the suitcase and go around his left wrist to capture the sun's glow. A miracle, the children thought. The family would then gaze after him – the walking, well-groomed, unbelievable marvel so like a whiteman – as he strutted down the fale steps on to the ground and out towards the town. Like an angel, or like a papalagi come to bring new hope into their miserable lives by showing them the marvellous and more civilised ways of the world, the envied whiteman's world.

Peilua would usually return at 6 o'clock sharp, undress, take another shower and, if he liked the look of the food, would eat while Tomasi and his family served, dress again in a clean sports shirt, clean trousers and socks, and newly-polished shoes, and go out once more. He would return at dawn to a bed of clean sheets (which he had brought back from New Zealand). He always locked the suitcase before going out at night to dazzle the men at Fofoga's shack, and the market billiard saloon, with his unlimited tales of the wonders of the world beyond the reefs, with his glittering attire and civilised manners. The men, awed by it all, paid for his drinks and loaned him money whenever he hinted at it.

Six months after Peilua returned, the Tomasi family woke up one rainy morning to find that Peilua had brought home a wife. (Most Vaipe marriages are common-law marriages: a couple simply decide to live together and have a family and that is marriage, it does not need the sanction of the law or the church. Only the members of the 'elite', or those who imagine themselves to be of that group, marry in church, pay for marriage licences and put on extravagant wedding-feasts which they can't really afford but which the Vaipe masses, who refer to themselves as the 'simple poor', thoroughly enjoy.) Mr and Mrs Tomasi were highly elated when they saw who Peilua had brought home. She was Luafata, daughter of Pavovale, one of the Vaipe elite who, a few years before, had been tragically shot by his wife for being unfaithful to her. Luafata was also beautiful and, like Peilua, was one of the most educated people in the Vaipe: she had nearly finished high school. After her father died and her mother was sent to prison, Luafata became a model of virtue, an example of what a 'good girl' should be.

The courtship hadn't been a lengthy one. Peilua, swooned over by nearly all the women in the Vaipe, had met her at a dance that night. After one dance (a waltz, was it?), which she considered an undreamed of privilege because Peilua was so much more beautiful and educated than her, she had followed him out of the dance hall, without her brothers knowing, and had gone home with him. When the news of Peilua's marriage broke, he (and Luafata) became the envy of the whole neighbourhood. Two such beautiful people, everyone said. Even her family, who should have assaulted Peilua for abducting Luafata their virginal daughter, were pleased about the marriage. Apart from Alapati, who had hoped that Peilua would marry a pastor's daughter, everyone else agreed that the marriage would be an exemplary one. The marriage was, so it would seem, a happy one for nearly a year.

In no way did the Tomasis feel exploited by Peilua and Luafata. Tomasi worked harder, getting a second job during the afternoons as a labourer on the wharf to feed, as it were, his nephew's expensive style of living. Luafata didn't go to work; she stayed home and took care of Peilua's possessions – the suitcase and its contents. Washed and ironed his clothes, polished his shoes and wrist-watch. He sometimes took her out to the movies, and that was enough for her. She always forgave him his infidelities which she heard about from gossips in the Vaipe. It was Peilua's right to be unfaithful; he was above all the vicious conventions observed by other people, she rationalised. Anyway, she was the one he really loved: she was the one he entrusted his suitcase to; he had even given her the other key to it, and she could spend hours examining the contents and Peilua wouldn't get angry. She never even got angry when Peilua started coming home drunk; she would undress him and put him into bed. She even accepted his slaps when she didn't wash or iron his clothes properly; she deserved his blows. One day he kicked her belly with a shoe-shod foot: she had torn a pocket off one of his shirts while washing it. She just wept. When he came home that night, she told him she was sorry and he forgave her. When he stopped making love to her altogether she didn't mind at all. He told her that she was 'too good' to make love to, and she believed him.

On the morning of Saturday, 23 December 1955, exactly one year after Peilua returned from New Zealand, Peilua and Luafata woke up to find that the suitcase had disappeared from underneath their bed. Peilua rushed out and kicked Tomasi and his family out of their sleep, shouting and raving unintelligibly, accusing everyone of having stolen the suitcase, 'his life' as he called it.

Mrs Tomasi and her children wept as they scrambled all round the fale, looking for the suitcase. Mr Tomasi tried to calm down Peilua, but got a vicious slap across the face, so he fled from the fale. Even Luafata got abused and slapped around and accused of having 'sent his life to her poverty-stricken family'.

When the suitcase wasn't found in or around the fale, Peilua ran to the Police Station, wearing only his bright red pair of shorts. It was the first time the neighbourhood saw him without his magnificent clothes. He returned with two puffing policemen, sat the policemen down, and then stormed around the fale, frantically explaining, in English, that 'some thieving bastard of a native had run off with his life'! Many of the neighbours had gathered round the fale. One of the policemen, a chunky corporal who secretly supported the nationalist movement, politely told him in aristocratic Samoan that both he and his colleague didn't understand English, so Peilua re-explained the whole story in Samoan and English. The corporal took down everything in Samoan in a thick notebook and, after promising in aristocratic Samoan that they would do their best to catch the 'patriotic Samoan' who had stolen Peilua's suitcase, left (never to be heard from again).

As soon as the policemen had gone, Peilua accused the inquisitive but sympathetic crowd of having stolen his suitcase. He told them, in extremely vile and ungentlemanly English, which most of the crowd didn't understand, that 'all Samoans were bloody thieves', that 'no whiteman would ever do a thing like that'. The crowd dispersed. Some of them, who understood English quite well, threatened to murder 'that palagi', namely Peilua.

Left alone with Mrs Tomasi and the children, who were all weeping profusely in the far side of the fale, and with Luafata who went over to him and, holding his bare arm, told him that she loved him even without his suitcase, Peilua crumpled on to the floor and wept bitterly, all the time saying, 'What am I going to do now? I've lost *every-thing!*' 'You've still got me', Luafata said to him. He pushed her away and sprang up to kick her, but she scrambled away across the fale. He sat down again and gazed into the floor mats, now and then sighing deeply and beating his brow with his clenched fists.

Night fell, and Luafata came to him and stood above him, hands on her hips, and said, 'Now you are nothing. I've had enough of you!'

'You can't leave me!' he said.

'Who said so. I hate you,' she said. He reached out for her hand but she slapped his hands away. 'I've had enough. Goodbye, whiteman!' she added in English.

She went back to her family and, like the two policemen, never came back.

Filled with liquor, Tomasi returned and told Peilua that if he, Peilua, didn't get a job by the end of the week he would have to go back to his father who deserved him.

'What about *our* bed?' his wife asked him.

'Yes,' Tomasi said to Peilua, 'from now on you sleep on the floor. We're taking our bed back, and our mats and mosquito net and curtain. From now on, you're just like us; you've got to pay your own way. There're no mosquitoes in this family!' (In the Vaipe, human parasites are called 'mosquitoes'.)

So from that day on – a day which has gone down in Vaipe history as 'The Day the Whiteman Lost His Life', Peilua slept on the hard floor on a humble mat, and without a mosquito net and under a thin sleeping sheet. But he still remained an optimist: every day he visited the Police Station to ask if they had found his suitcase. He even tried looking for a job. Many labouring jobs were available, but he wasn't ever going to dirty his hands. An office job befitting his elite rank was what he was after. He tried getting Luafata back but, every time he approached her, she told him to go look for 'his life' somewhere else.

During the next few months after his suitcase was stolen, Peilua never went out at night, and he avoided meeting any of his former friends (and they were numerous) to whom he owed money. Everywhere he went in the Vaipe, the young people called him 'the naked whiteman'. He grew thin, because Tomasi no longer fed him elite food and went out of his way to abuse him verbally, calling him a 'good-for-nothing layabout'. His one remaining sports shirt soon lost its colour and grew holes which went unpatched because he didn't know how to sew. So did his remaining pair of trousers and his one pair of socks and shoes. He kept them as clean as possible and wore them only when he went looking for work. At home, he wore an old lavalava and singlet which Tomasi had given him grudgingly. He wasn't really hurt by it all: he was eagerly expecting his father to plead with him to return home and live out again the style of living his father had brought him up to expect.

The morning before he died, Alapati sent for Peilua and laid the curse upon him for all time.

That night, Peilua put on his sports shirt, trousers, socks and shoes and went to Fofoga's shack.

He stopped at the threshold. The crowded room fell silent.

'Come in, whiteman!' Fofoga, the obese man behind the makeshift bar, called to him in English.

Peilua went in. Everyone watched him as he moved up to the bar. 'You don't look so good, fellow,' said Fofoga, pouring him a glass of beer. Peilua picked up the glass and drank until the glass was empty. He felt the other men shifting closer to him. An elbow jolted into his side. He took no notice of it. 'Another glass?' asked Fofoga. Peilua nodded. A small ball of paper hit him on the back of his head and bounced past Fofoga. Fofoga poured him another beer. 'Now pay up,' Fofoga said. Peilua took the full glass out of Fofoga's hand and drank the beer in it in one long swallow. He replaced the empty glass on the bar and motioned to Fofoga to fill it again. Fofoga looked at the other men, at Lafoga, one of Luafata's older brothers who was notorious in the Vaipe for violence. Lafoga nodded to Fofoga. Fofoga refilled Peilua's glass. Again Peilua drank until it was empty.

As he was putting the glass down another elbow jolted into his right side. This time it was harder to ignore it because everyone had seen it done, but Peilua ignored it. He turned slowly and faced the men sitting around dirty tables and on the floor. They were like images in a dream, silent and threatening, ready to assume illogical patterns of violence he wouldn't be able to understand; and, in not comprehending them, he would become mortally afraid of them. But he sensed – delving desperately into the memories of the Vaipe world that had existed for him before he had gone away to New Zealand – what they wanted of him and from him. He had betrayed them by betraying himself. He had betrayed their hopes and dreams which they had wanted him to live out for them.

'Forgive me,' he said. No one said anything. 'Forgive me. I didn't mean to . . . . '

'To what?' said Lafoga, who was now standing beside him.

And there it was – the final choice. Peilua hesitated and his courage died. 'Nothing,' he said. He turned to the bar again, his back to them. Lafoga laughed challengingly in his ear. 'Please!' Peilua murmured.

He wheeled to run out of the shack.

Two men blocked his way. Turned to his left. Two other men.

'Please!' Peilua pleaded, crumpling to his knees. 'Please, I didn't mean to do it to her. I loved her. Hear me, I loved her but she was unfaithful to me!'

And what he had tried for a year now to hide from his conscience broke out to confront him. Mary Dunstan, that was her name, the papalagi woman he had fallen in love with in New Zealand, and to whom he had given all his trust, but who had betrayed him as he had betrayed the Vaipe that he had known and loved in his childhood. He would have done anything for her. Anything. When he first met her, she symbolised, for him, everything that he was searching for in her world: beauty, goodness, gentleness, learning, sexual freedom. How mistaken he had been about her! So wrong.

He had found her in bed with another man. He nearly killed her and her lover, beating them with his fists in an outburst of mad courage, a courage which she had taken from him when he had fallen in love with her.

The judge ruled that he be deported.

Now as he knelt and pleaded with these men, with the Vaipe, asking that he be forgiven for something they didn't understand or want to understand, he knew that he still loved her. He also knew that he was too afraid to accept the final judgement of the Vaipe.

So he wept in fear.

He screamed when strong, cruel hands gripped his arms and lifted him up to his feet. Sobbed when the first fist crunched into his face and he staggered back, blood streaming from his nose.

They beat him until he was unconscious, removed his shirt, trousers and shoes, and then hurled him out of the shack into the night.

He spent twelve weeks in hospital after undergoing a difficult brain operation: extensive brain damage had been caused when he had landed on rocks in front of the shack. His older brother went to the hospital and brought him home.

Peilua is still alive in the Vaipe. If you want to see him, you'll find him sitting on a filthy canvas chair under the breadfruit trees in front of his family's fale. He is only thirty-five years old, but he looks like a wizened old man, with arthritic hands and grey hair and a timeless, trusting gaze in his deepset eyes. Go and ask him who he is.

He'll tell you in English: 'I am white. A whiteman.' And smile like a contented child.

The true son of the Vaipe died in New Zealand, killed by a woman who didn't love him. A whiteman was deported to the Vaipe. We crucified him.

# Declaration of Independence

Mr Paovale Iosua, utterly loyal Senior Clerk of the Public
Works Department, having been a junior and then senior
clerk there for over thirty-two years, stern father of seven
normal children (four boys and three girls), respected if, at
times, over-zealous and pompous deacon in the Apia
Congregational Church, dedicated if somewhat pedestrian
chairman of the local Boys' Brigade, faithful member of
the Avele Old Boys' Association and an avid compulsive
reader of fundamentalist religious pamphlets disseminated
by Jehovah's Witnesses, was having a leisurely morning
shave under the shower behind his fale (and, although sixty
years old, was feeling that he was capable of living forever)
when Nofoa, his wife of over forty years and mother of all
his children, slipped through the hibiscus hedge surrounding
the shower and, after asking him if he was enjoying his
shave, blew his brains out with a shotgun which her
neighbour, Mrs Tanielu, had so conveniently lent her the
night before. (Mrs Tanielu, two days before, had informed
Nofoa that her husband was sending gifts of perfume and
extra-large pieces of silk material to a young 'half-Chinese
hussy' who worked in his office. Such presents, concluded
Mrs Tanielu – whom Paovale had refused to marry forty
years before – can only mean one thing: adultery. 'What can
be more *intimate* and tempting than perfume!' Mrs Tanielu
had exclaimed.)

Nofoa, whom Paovale had loved fervently – from the
minute he had first discovered (under a hedge a street
away from Motootua Hospital where she was studying to

be a nurse) that she was a virgin to the instant she killed him – was not a violent person. All the witnesses at her trial agreed on this point. Everyone in her neighbourhood, church, and Women's Committee considered her lovable, loving, and absolutely devoted to her husband, children, family, and God. At her trial, her pastor, Faasami Luapo, who believed in capital punishment, declared: 'Nofoa is very, very honest; very kind, very hard-working. A very, very loyal daughter of the church. She is not capable of harming anyone'. But Judge Macarthy, a decrepit Scotsman with fiery red hair and an Old-Testament voice which had earned him the nickname 'The Devil', was not interested in past performance, as it were. 'I am willing to believe – in fact, I *do* believe – that Mrs Paovale is a good mother, an honest and charitable Christian and a worthy citizen; but all that has nothing to do with the price of murder!' proclaimed Judge Macarthy from under his white wig. 'According to the Prosecution, Mrs Paovale murdered her husband, one Paovale Iosua, in cold blood'.

The next day, the Court, which was Judge Macarthy, concluded that Mrs Paovale had killed her husband in a fit of jealousy; she had killed him with two shots from a 12-gauge shotgun; she had then, of her own volition, given herself up to the Police and had, in a written confession, admitted to having killed one Paovale Iosua. Mrs Paovale, aged fifty-eight, of the Vaipe, was therefore guilty of premeditated murder.

Most of the people at her trial concluded that Mrs Paovale had killed her husband because he had been unfaithful to her – a very justifiable reason for killing him. Any wife or husband who didn't react in like manner to infidelity or cuckoldry was neither male or female but spineless. To have blown out his unfaithful brains with a shotgun was extremely fitting; to have given herself up to the Police, and confessed all, was truly grand, heroic, and Christian. Mrs Nofoa Paovale, aged fifty-eight, of the Vaipe, was therefore not guilty of premeditated murder: she had, in a very apt and proper manner, righted a grievous wrong committed against her by one Paovale Iosua, aged sixty, of the Vaipe.

Late that afternoon, 4 p.m. on 15th February, 1952, the Court, which was Judge Macarthy, otherwise known as 'The Fly-Shitted-Faced Devil' because of his uncountable freckles, found Mrs Nofoa Paovale guilty of murder and sentenced her to be hanged.

Another hot day: Paovale knew that even before he was fully awake. Temperatures in the eighties, no wind, and all pulsating sun. The secret was in his skin – extra sensitive it was, like the most accurate thermometer. Every morning now, as far back as he cared to remember, he could *feel* what kind of day it was going to be before opening his eyes. 6.30 or 6.35 a.m., he knew that too without having to look at the watch under his pillow. He always woke on the dot, needed no alarm clock; the clock was in his head, wired to the nerves of his brain after thirty years of habitually waking at that time. He opened his eyes. Sighed. 1st June 1951, and he was sixty years, five months, twenty days old. He sat up in the mosquito net and, without looking around him, knew exactly where every member of his family was at that moment: Nofoa and his high school daughters were in the kitchen fale preparing breakfast – tea, bread, and butter; the older boys were in and around the shower, getting ready for work, and their wives were helping in the kitchen fale; Malelua, his youngest and favourite son (whom he hoped would someday complete high school and acquire a government scholarship to New Zealand and return with a university degree) was still asleep in the only bed in the fale; his five grandsons were under Malelua's bed; his four granddaughters were either outside picking up the fallen breadfruit leaves, or still sleeping. Yawning loudly, Paovale pulled up the side of the net, edged out of it on his haunches and sat cross-legged, facing the road now awake with traffic, sleeping sheet wrapped around his body. The stench of the Vaipe – the stream which flowed past the fale only a few yards away behind blooming hibiscus and neat rows of taro, and after which the neighbourhood was called – saturated the morning air, but he was used to it, having accepted it, in his childhood, as a vital part of his acre of land, fale, family, and neighbourhood. Like the odour of death, he had thought often, when late at night he would sit listening to the stream shifting, a solid snake of mud, out past the Police Station towards Mulivai Cathedral and the sea.

He started singing the hymn for morning prayers, and his grandsons and Malelua woke up with coughs and sniffs and joined in the singing. 6.45 a.m. He said a short prayer, got up, rehitched his lavalava, folded his sleeping sheet and placed it gingerly on the varnished wooden trunk behind the net, and then went out to shower.

All his married sons were gathered around the open fire in the kitchen fale, drinking steaming mugs of tea and eating thick slices of bread, while Nofoa and his daughters-in-law were buttering more slices of bread and piling them on to tin plates, ready for the school children to eat. His eldest sons were a bitter disappointment to him. None of them had gone past standard two at the Malifa Primary School, and it wasn't *his* fault. He had done his best to try and get them interested in a good education and the Government office jobs which such an education would have given them, but they had simply chosen the streets of Apia, the billiard saloons, the movie theatre and the home-brew dens – the easy, jobless gaiety and life of most of the Vaipe youth, until they found themselves with wives, and, tired of supporting them completely, Paovale had got them work as roadmenders with the Public Works. He was still supporting them, it was his duty to do so, they were his children, the God-given blessing he had to bear until he retired – which was only two years away – and then they would have to support him. Malelua, the brilliant son, would, with his university degree, provide him with a comfortable retirement and higher status and prestige in the Vaipe and in the country.

His daughters came out of the shower, and, as they passed him, acknowledged him with curt nods. Sina, the oldest girl, who was extremely attractive and obedient, wanted to be a nurse; Faatasi, the ugly one, wanted to be a teacher; and Luafata, as yet, didn't know what she wanted to do. They were all doing well at school. All of them would marry well, he hoped. To pastors perhaps. Or papalagi. Or teachers. Or

Samoan doctors. Or, if it had to be, to local highly-placed civil servants. Marriage to such men would give them self-respect and status. So many Vaipe girls had drifted, and were drifting, into what he called 'the sinful life'. No self-respect. Whores all! He stopped himself from thinking about it any further. He went into the shower.

Before turning on the shower, he gazed up into the sky now ablaze with a vigorous, mushrooming light. What a shame I can't stop working and simply be an old man sitting peacefully in the shade, waiting to die and not worrying about protecting anyone, just a contented spirit ready to go to God. He could feel the power of the sky embracing him gently, sucking him up. He turned on the shower without thinking and the cold drenched him, shocked him back down into the reality of his life – the stench of urine rising from the rock floor of the shower, the earthworms wriggling up through the mud at the foot of the hedge, and the flies and the mounting, brittle cold in his bones. But I imagine not, he thought. He was tied to the earth, chained to it by the inescapable currents emanating from the warmth out of which he had come; the earth drawing him back into it, as the sky had attempted to lift him up like a fragment of light, a nimble star. He got the razor from the small steel shelf attached to the shower and started shaving, nonchalantly. You, Paovale Iosua, his father would have said, are a sixty-year-old civil servant who has no right to fancy visions or dreams; you have a large, hungry, greedy family to feed, clothe, educate and perhaps bury; you have to continue selling your blood to keep alive the fruit of your flesh, keep them kicking and laughing and fornicating to produce more mouths to gnaw at the marrow of your bones until you are finally an empty, dry pod; you, my son, are a little man, a starched-clothed Government employee worthy only of your $60 a month, a meagre pension when you retire, and a not-too-expensive wooden coffin – hammered together haphazardly by your ungrateful and worthless sons – when you stop breathing and start smelling like Vaipe mud. Paovale flung the razor at the hedge. But what were you! he cursed the memory of his father. You couldn't carry the family burden. You died clutching a toothless, syphilitic whore. You inherited eight acres of Vaipe land which you sold to pay your debts, to pay for drinks and women. You betrayed our family. You were a man without honour, morals, strength, or God. I may be a small man but I have honour and self-respect. I have done my duty to the family. I pay my debts. I have God. *You may have God, son, but you're still a little man. A small man, weak even down there where a man should be able to stand up and fight valiantly. When was the last time you sharpened your weapon? A year ago, two years, a decade ago? Poor, son, just a pitifully shrivelled-up banana!*

Paovale showered quickly, frantically, inwardly cursing his father and himself and the life that could have been his, cursing his family, cursing his job, with the water hissing and spitting down at him and shattering on him into droplets which sprayed all around him and, in the now brilliant light, glinted like tiny drops of mercury or sparks flashing out of a smokeless fire, making him appear as if he was burning.

Nofoa was waiting for him with his breakfast when he returned from the shower. He stamped into the fale, whipped off his wet lavalava from underneath the dry towel which he had wrapped on, flung it out on to the stone paepae, and then disappeared behind the curtains to start dressing for work.

'What's the matter?' she called to him. No reply. She poured herself a mug of tea and started eating her breakfast. Apart from the toddlers, who were now in the kitchen fale being fed by their respective mothers, all the other children had left for school.

'Where's my lavalava?' he called.

'In the trunk,' she replied.

'And my shirt?'

'Same place.'

'Find them!'

She went through the curtains and got the clothes from the trunk and handed them to him. He was combing his hair in front of the mirror attached to the tallboy. He ignored her. She placed the clothes on top of the trunk and turned to go.

'Handkerchief?'

She got a white one out of the trunk and put it with his clothes.

'Tie?'

She got that out of the trunk too. He turned from the mirror and, without looking at her standing there trying not to be impatient with him, dismissed her with an abrupt wave. Flinging her hands up in growing exasperation, she turned and went to finish her breakfast.

'My sandals?' he called just as she was sitting down.

'What about them?'

'Where are they?'

Trying not to shout, she replied: 'Behind the trunk, on the floor.' There was a loud clatter of the trunk being flung aside, a muffled curse, then the banging of sandals being slapped against the trunk. She continued eating. After a further series of curses in a mixture of English and Samoan, more bangs, clatters, and deep sighs, he came out and stood in front of the curtains and glared at his wife and his breakfast and the world.

He was dressed in his navy-blue tie, starched-white shirt with the frayed collar and foodstains down the front, cream-coloured tailor-made lavalava with pockets, and he wore thick-soled sandals shiny black with care and age.

'Don't be childish!' she said.

He blinked. 'Childish? Childish?' he muttered.

'Yes, childish,' she said. 'Come and eat. You'll be late for work.'

'That's all I get in this house – ingratitude. No one looks after my clothes properly. To all of you, I'm just a nobody, a fool . . . . You're all killing me!'

'Sit down and eat,' she said. He sat down, talking still. She pushed his breakfast towards him.

' . . . I work my heart out and what do I get? Eh, what? Nothing but ingratitude. Oh, what's the use!' He continued ranting loud enough to instil fear into his daughters-in-law in the kitchen fale. 'All my life – work, work, and work! What for? Nothing. I'm old and sick and tired . . . . ' Nofoa had heard it all before and, knowing that it was one of his usual ways of attracting attention and sympathy, she didn't get angry. He'd finish raving, get up obediently and go off to work. He would do nothing rash, foolish or violent. Paovale was Paovale: a quiet, harmless, conscientious provider, a good husband; that's why she loved him. Most Vaipe husbands didn't work at all, many because of lack of work but mostly because they didn't want to work; they beat their wives mercilessly, got drunk often, lay with other women, stole, brawled, and broke every other commandment in the Holy Book; they neglected their families and church. Just like the ignorant, pagan savages of the pre-Christian days all living in dark sin and fear. Paovale was none of these: he was gentle, kind, *civilised*.

'Jam?' he asked her.

'None,' she said.

'No jam?'

'No, none. The children finished . . . .

'See what I mean? I get nothing, nothing, nothing!' Grabbing his mug of tea he hurled it out of the fale. He sprang up and kicked the plate of bread: the slices scattered and the plate sailed over Nofoa's head and landed on Malelua's bed. 'Sick, sick, sick! I'm sick of – oh, hell!' Wheeling, he thumped down the two front steps and stalked, across the lawn now stiff with sun, towards the road.

'Your briefcase!' she called.

He stopped and, without turning around, shouted, 'Bring it!'

She took it to him.


Past the Police Station, a sprawling double-storey building with spacious verandas and dust-caked walls (with a few policemen whom he knew sitting in the sun on the front veranda), sandals crunching on the gravel pavement, kicking up puffs of dust which clung to the bottom edge of his lavalava. Past the Treasury building, another double-storey structure of wood and whitewash facing the harbour, until, turning left, he was on Beach Road, the town's main street hugging the shoreline and disappearing into the heart of Apia like a dry river bed, and he glanced at the harbour, at the swelling sea still bare of ships and boats and which rolled away gently to a horizon of kapok-white cloud holding up the sky's edge. Past the small grimy fire-station, to which he sometimes came at night to play cards with the bored firemen who rarely got fires to extinguish, acknowledging now with a broad smile the verbal greetings of two young firemen sitting on the veranda railing. Past the market – grey steel pillars supporting a dome of rusting corrugated iron under which milling pedlars of seafood, fruit and vegetables were already setting up stalls and laughing and arguing as if they owned the town, now smelling of exhaust fumes, stale food and rubbish, unwashed bodies and sun. Past a few more wooden buildings, all stores huddled shoulder to shoulder, display windows gaping at him. Then to the northern entrance into the heart of the Vaipe neighbourhood, a narrow alleyway between two stores and guarded by over-flowing piles of rubbish buzzing with swarms of flies, where, without thinking, he stopped for a moment and looked through the entrance at the dilapidated fale and shacks grouped around a small malae covered with black pebbles and stones, at a forgotten world cut off from the sea and sun, the miserable world which had become his inheritance after his forefathers had sold all the valuable land on which the town now stood. Sold it for axes, tobacco, muskets and calico to papalagi traders (or gave much of it to the Church). Paovale was no longer bitter about it, having, years before, accepted – because he couldn't do anything else but accept – the miserly hand which a history of ignorance and greed and falsehood and double-dealing had dealt him. God will eventually put things right, he thought as he walked on. His anger, connected with his family, had ebbed away and he walked lightly, once again the Mr Paovale Iosua whom he (and most of the people who knew him) had come to believe he was – armoured in starched-white, right hand gripping firmly the handle of his black leather briefcase which had his name etched on it in gold lettering – an important Government official, proud and loyal servant of the colonial power, fluent in both languages, whose children were doing extremely well at the best Government school, a kind, uprighteous husband and father, an indomitable Christian citizen. Alive, contented and ready to carry out the colonial Government's business.

He went up the aisle between the rows of office desks. The chattering group of typists and clerks at the far end of the room stopped talking and scattered to their respective desks when they saw him. Taking a bunch of keys out of his pocket, he opened the door into the small glass compartment which was his office and went in. He put his briefcase on the desk, sat down in the swivel chair and gazed out into the outer office at the backs of the typists and clerks who were now working with exaggerated enthusiasm. The desks, shelves and louvre windows gleamed with sunlight. All chromium and varnish and orderly and tidy. When he was satisfied that everything (and everyone) was functioning normally, he opened his briefcase. Out of it came two pencils, three ball-point pens and a Parker 51 pen, which he put carefully on the right-hand edge of the layer of blotting paper on his desk. Then he placed the briefcase on the shelves behind him, pulled open the top drawers of his desk, flicked through the piles of papers and accounts in them, found the files he wanted and spread them out on the blotting paper. Wiped his hands on his lavalava, stretched his fingers, his knuckles cracking audibly, picked up the Parker 51 pen, uncapped it, examined the nib, nodded, opened the top file, sighed, and then started working. No wasted effort, every action was part of a ritual refined and perfected over the years until it had become part of him, part of the greater ritual which was his life.

An hour passed. Sums of money checked, noted and balanced. Noted and balanced. Neat little figures which protected him and held him in a womb, safe from the turbulent world beyond the glass walls of his office. Another hour, then the soft knocking on the door. He didn't need to look up to know who it was: Mrs Tina Meyer, the senior typist, part-German office gossip who was childless, over-talkative, at times bumptious, but harmless; in awe of his position as those junior to her were in awe of hers, and so on down the methodical, orderly ladder of seniority which he (and the Colonial Government) had created within those walls (and in all other government departments). He motioned to her to enter.

'Good morning,' she said in English. (He didn't allow the use of Samoan during working hours.)

He got a sheaf of letters, which he had written the day before, out of the bottom left-hand drawer and gave it to her. 'Make sure the girls use good English, correct spelling and so on,' he said to her. (He told her this every morning.) She nodded and clutched the letters to her abundant bosom as if she was ready to guard them with her life.

'Anything else?' she asked. He looked at her. 'Anything else, sir?' she corrected her error.

Smiling benevolently, he said, 'No.' She backed out of the room.

He glanced at his watch. 10.30 a.m. He closed the accounts on his desk, got up, inserted the accounts into the top drawer of the metal filing cabinet near his desk, quickly straightened the papers and pens on his desk, brushed back his hair with his hands, straightened his tie, and then, with measured steps, strolled out into the main office, hands clutched behind his back.

The murmuring stopped as he went from desk to desk, peering over the shoulders of the typists and clerks, saying nothing but now and then pointing accusingly at a mis-spelt word, a grammatical mistake, a wrong addition or an untidy page, the culprit mumbling sorry sir and promising to correct the error, promptly.

When he reached the waist-high swing door that opened out into the main corridor, he turned and like an emperor surveying his empire, gazed benignly at the typists and clerks and the office furniture and at the windows all golden with sun. Perfect order, efficiency, cleanliness, and hard-work were virtues second only to Godliness, he thought.

Behind him, across the corridor and attached to the wall, was a red-tiled staircase which led up to the spacious offices of the Director and the Assistant Director, a realm forbidden to all employees apart from Mr Paovale and personnel of his rank. When he heard footsteps echoing down the stairs, he straightened and turned to confront the staircase with a beaming smile.

Mr David Trust, Assistant Director, hit the bottom step

94

and marched towards him, big feet shod in shiny brown leather shoes which thudded across the concrete floor in a military display of confident ownership, benenevolent overlordship, and paternalistic possession of everything (including Mr Paovale Iosua) around him. After all, Western Samoa was a colony of New Zealand and Mr Trust's country was New Zealand and he was a high-ranking New Zealand official here to help civilise these people and thereby make them worthy of independence and the modern world.

'Good morning,' Mr Trust said to Paovale, looking over Paovale's head into the office beyond.

'Morning, sir,' replied Paovale, almost coming to attention.

'Everything all right? No problems?' Mr Trust was extremely lanky, sinewy, and sharp-faced, with a thin mouth nearly blocked from view by a hooked nose. Skin was flaking off his cheeks and nose. He had straight black hair parted on the right side and slicked down over his small head with liquid vaseline hair-oil. And he smelled of sun after spending the previous week-end trying to acquire a tan. To Paovale, everything about Mr Trust was wonderfully and enviously papalagi, civilised.

'No, sir,' replied Paovale.

'Good. Very good.' Mr Trust always spoke very crisply and precisely in an attempt to disguise, if not hide, his very nasal, very harsh New Zealand accent, an accent which he had tried to lose while working as a clerk in the New Zealand Armed Forces in Italy during the Second World War. With Paovale, he needn't have bothered: Paovale adored his accent and wanted his son Malelua to speak English just like Mr Trust.

Paovale swung open the swing door. Mr Trust stepped through and, standing beside Paovale who only came up to his shoulder, surveyed the office in one sweeping glance. 'Oh, by the way, there's a new typist coming to work for you at 11.30 this morning. A Miss Anna Che .... Never mind, she'll tell you her own name. Girl's Chinese. Young, a good worker according to her school reports.'

'Thank you, sir.'

'Right,' said Mr Trust. Then, in long military strides,

started going round the office with Paovale following one precise pace behind him.

Mr Paovale (he was a Mister again now that Mr David Trust, a superior Mister, had left) went into his office and had his morning tea – two crisp gingernut biscuits and a cup of tea without milk, exactly what the Director had for his morning tea. (Mrs Meyer had put it on his desk.) Paovale, like Mr Trust and the Director, always had his morning tea alone and in his office, the rest of the staff had theirs together around the office-boy's desk. Fifteen minutes was the prescribed length of time for morning tea, and, when it was up, the office-boy, a swarthy middle-aged man dressed in starched-white shirt, shorts and knee-high socks, came and collected the empty cup and saucer.

11.30 a.m. Mr Paovale put the files away in his desk and, while waiting for the new typist, scribbled aimlessly on a pad.

Mrs Meyer knocked and entered. He continued scribbling without looking up at her. 'Yes?' he asked, knowing already why she had come.

'There's a girl to see you, sir,' she said.

'A Chinese girl?'

'Yes, sir. A Chinese girl.'

'Send her in.' He ripped off the top page, screwed it up, dropped it into the waste-paper basket by his desk and pretended to be writing something very important on the next page.

He didn't look up when she came in. 'Sit down,' he said. The chair opposite him creaked and he caught the pleasant smell of perfume. He scribbled on. 'What can I do for you?'

A frightened pause, then she said, hesitantly, 'I was sent by Mr Trust.' A very palagi, very melodious voice, he concluded. Like Mrs Ethel Trust's voice.

'You're the new typist?'

'Yes.'

'In this office of Government we address our superior as *sir*,' he said, looking at her for the first time.

'I'm sorry, sir,' she said, gazing down at her hands clasped in her lap. Very attractive for a part-Chinese, he thought. Must be her Samoan blood. Nothing like it to make beautiful the ugly Oriental features.

'Name?' he asked, the sternness gone out of his voice.

'Anna Chan, sir,' she said. He wrote it down. A very palagi face, he noted. Prominent cheekbones, thin nose not too long, faint trace of Chinese in the eyes, black eyelashes and hair shiny with perfumed hair-oil, a perfectly palagi mouth beautiful with lipstick. Nearly as beautiful as Mrs Trust.

'Age?'

'Nineteen, sir.'

'Good, good,' he said, writing it down. Expensive white blouse with frilly lace round the neck and sleeve edges, expensive blue skirt tight round the hips and barely covering her knees, expensive silver wrist-watch and bangles. As beautiful as Mrs Ethel Trust.

'Where did you go to school?'

'To the Mormon College, sir.'

'A Mormon?'

'I'm sorry, sir.' She was frightened again and he cursed his stupidity.

'Nevermind. I have nothing against Mormons. I have many, many friends who are Mormons. People are people. As long as a person goes to church I have nothing against him. Or her. I'm L.M.S. myself,' he said. She smiled, and he felt good inside, warm and glad that he had healed the *unreasonable* hurt he had inadvertently dealt her. She was Chinese and a Mormon but she was so like Mrs Ethel Trust, his ideal woman, wife and mother. 'What does your father do?' he found himself asking her. She frowned and he immediately regretted having asked.

'He has a business,' she said. He sensed at once that she was ashamed of her father, and he sympathised with her. What girl-child wanted an indentured Chinese labourer for a father!

'Nevermind. We can't help what our parents were. Or are,' he said.

Smiling, she said, 'He owns a few taxis and a restaurant.'

'You mean, *the* Mr Chan?'

'Yes, sir.'

'I'm glad. I know your father quite well.' Mr Chan was one of the wealthiest businessmen in the country. He had come to Samoa as an indentured plantation labourer working for only 10 sene a day. And now, even though he still couldn't read or write or speak English or Samoan properly, he owned a fleet of taxis, a thriving restaurant, two cacao plantations and a modern double-storey general store. 'It'll be a privilege having the daughter of one of our country's most respected citizens working in our department. You may start work right away if you want to, *Miss* Chan.'

'Thank you, sir,' she said.

He motioned to Mrs Meyer. She came quickly. 'Take Miss Chan and give her a good desk, one of our best typewriters and so on. She starts work today,' he instructed Mrs Meyer. Miss Chan got up. 'Oh, and from now on let Miss Chan type all my correspondence. She's the most qualified of all our young typists.' Mrs Meyer looked hurt and offended, but he didn't notice.

'Thank you, sir,' said Miss Chan. She followed Mrs Meyer out into the main office.

His glass-walled office would never be the same again. Miss Chan had come. The vitality and beauty and innocence of youth, he thought. Like dawn, or warm sunlight lacing gold into the morning sea. Miss Chan, *Miss Anna Chan*, such a melodious name, so like the vibrant and vital Mrs Ethel Trust: the world of the papalagi he had desired all his miserable life, the essence of youth he had never possessed, the throbbing, exhilarating strength he had discovered in Nofoa when he had first married her. He sat at his desk, scribbling on the pad until lunchtime, scribbling and savouring, in his mind, every detail of his interview with Miss Anna Chan and now and then gazing out at her and sighing.

Before leaving for home and his lunch of boiled breadfruit and tinned herrings, he persuaded himself that, being a godly and faithful husband, there was nothing sinful in his idealisation of Miss Chan and Mrs Trust. Nothing sexual, or unclean.

Mr Trust was named David John by his domineering mother who had divorced his father after thirty years of being married to 'that failed dairy farmer' who had failed to provide her with a permanent five-bedroom house, a car, a washing machine, carpets on the floor, and all those other possessions that reasonable wives had a right to expect from reasonable husbands. Mr Trust had been in Western Samoa for nearly four years. After the War, he had returned to his position as clerk with the New Zealand State Advances Corporation and had worked there for another two years before applying for a job in the Samoan Civil Service. He got his present position because no other New Zealander had applied for it. He was married (and had been married for nearly fifteen years) to a woman five years older than himself. Ethel, his wife, had been a school-teacher in a small country town. On a deer-stalking expedition with some of his office friends, he had met her in a little pub in the lonely town where she taught and had, after a wild party which had started soon after he had bought her a whisky, made love to her on the sofa of her little house. (He would always be disappointed that she hadn't been a virgin.) A month later, after a series of what they in their adolescence would have called 'love letters', they got married in the big Methodist church in a big suburb of what they called 'his city', Auckland. He married her, so he later came to reason to himself, because no other woman had ever looked at him twice let alone permitted him to make love to her more than once in the span of a few days. When he was with his friends (all New Zealanders in the Samoan Administration), he referred to her as 'that wonderful woman': but in private, and not to her face because he was terrified of her, he labelled her 'that nagging frigid bitch'. Every year just before Christmas, after nearly 365 days of her, he always contemplated asking her for a divorce. They had three children – two boys and a girl, whom he didn't feel close to. Ethel had wanted three children: the first one three years after they got married, the second one four years after that, and the last one five years after that. He had complied.

Mr and Mrs Trust were members of the predominantly papalagi Anglican Church, the exclusively white Returned Servicemen's Association, the mainly expatriate Apia Golf Club and Turf Club and Yacht Club, the expatriate-controlled Red Cross, and the impeccably Victorian Chess

Club. Mrs Trust was also dominant in the Overseas Wives' Club and Women's Guild. They had a large, well-furnished Government house, a garden boy who was in his sixties, two house-girls, who both had husbands, a dog, which had been castrated, a cat, which had been spayed, and two budgies, because there were no birds in Samoa which looked like birds.


'You've been out with her again, haven't you?' she asked. He continued eating, without replying or looking at her. The children were asleep; she had been waiting up until midnight for him to come home. 'Haven't you?' she repeated. He nodded. 'But why her?'

He dropped his fork on to the plate. 'Because she lets me.'

'But she's . . . she's . . . . '

'Chinese and coloured?' he interrupted her.

'Yes.'

'You hate *them*, don't you, dear?'

'Yes. But so do you!'

He got up slowly, picked up his plate, took it and left it on the gleaming sink-bench, and then, turning to her sitting there at the dinner table, hands clutched to her face, said, 'She may be Chinese and coloured, and I may hate *them*, but she makes me feel like a man. At least in bed.' This was the first time he had been unfaithful to her.

'I'm going to leave you, David,' she said.

'Go ahead.' He was a complete stranger to her. He had always been utterly faithful and obedient, but adultery seemed to have changed him into a defiant, reckless stranger.

'What about the kids?' she asked.

'What about them?'

'They're yours!'

'You can have them.' He went into the bathroom. She followed him hurriedly, fearfully.

'You must never see that Chinese bitch again!' she said to him from the doorway. 'I forbid you to!' He brushed his teeth noisily. 'If you see her again, I'm going to . . . . ' She stopped, too afraid to say it in case he agreed to it.

'Divorce me, Ethel,' was all he said, his back still turned to her.

'You'd like that, wouldn't you? It's the easy way out for you, so you can continue doing that bitch, and I'd be left with your bloody kids!'

'So, don't divorce me.' He wiped his hands and mouth on the towel, brushed past her and went into their bedroom across the passage.

He was undressing in front of the wardrobe mirror when she came into the bedroom. She sat down on the bed and started sobbing quietly into her hands.

'Why are you doing this to me?' she said.

'Doing what?' he asked, flinging his underpants into the far corner of the room.

'Humiliating me.' She looked up and saw him scratching his genitals and gazing into the mirror.

'Because you've been humiliating me for the past fifteen years.' He pulled on a pair of blue pyjama pants and sat down on the bed behind her.

'But how?'

'You know how.' He rolled down the bedcover and lay down on the bed.

'You mean the sex part of our marriage?'

'You put it so well, Ethel.'

She glanced over her shoulder at him. His eyes were closed. 'Is . . . is she good?' she asked hesitantly but surprised at her own bold curiosity.

'Yes, *very* good.'

'I mean, in bed?'

'That's what I meant.' He rolled on to his left shoulder, his back to her.

'How long has it been going on?'

' 'Bout four months. Yes, four *beautiful* months. Ever since she came to work.' He sounded so proud and pleased about it that she sprang up and ran out of the bedroom and on to the outside veranda.

She returned to the bedroom in the early hours of the morning. Standing above him in the darkness, she said, 'I hate you. I hate her. I hate this . . . yes, this *fucken* country!' She started caressing his shoulder. 'Oh, David, I want to go back *home*. Take me home, David.' He was fast asleep.

On the bright Tuesday morning, three days before the office broke up for the 1951 Christmas holidays, Mr Paovale, after dictating letters to Miss Anna Chan, gave her his fatal present – three yards of expensive but genuine Hong Kong silk and a bottle of brilliantine perfume. He was dead a week later. Neither the Director of Public Works, nor Mr David Trust nor Miss Anna Chan attended his funeral; the office-boy delivered a wreath of plastic flowers bought by Mrs Tina Meyer who a month later was promoted by Mr Trust to Paovale's desk and swivel chair in the small glass office. The Trust family left hurriedly for New Zealand fòur nerve racking months after. (David remained married to Ethel until he died of a heart-attack sixteen years later. To that eventful day he was never again unfaithful to her.) Miss Anna Chan gave birth to an eight-pound, sandy-haired, green-eyed boy a few months after Mr Trust left the colony. (She never again trusted promises of papalagi men, especially in relation to divorcing their frigid wives and marrying her.)

Mrs Paovale was not hanged: the Colonial Governor commuted her sentence to life imprisonment. She was released on the first day of the new year, 1962, when the Head of State of the newly independent State of Western Samoa signed a general amnesty freeing all prisoners to mark Western Samoa's first Independence Day. She is still living in the Vaipe. She visits her husband's grave at Magiagi Cemetery every Saturday afternoon.

# Flying-Fox in a Freedom Tree

There is a buzzing fly in my hospital room. It is hitting against the wire screen all the time, killing itself slowly. 10 o'clock in the morning. A hot sun is coming through the windows on to the foot of my bed. Through the window I see the plain on which this hospital stands, dropping down to the ravine, and on the other side the land rises up through taro and banana patches and mango and tamaligi trees to palms at the top of the range. Further up the range, Robert Louis Stevenson is buried there. (If my novel is as good as Stevenson's *Treasure Island*, I will be satisfied.) I had breakfast. A cup of tea, a piece of toast. They tasted like a stale horse or something. On the ravine edge stands a shed surrounded by mounds of dry coconut husks. The shed has no walls and I can see (as I have seen for the last three months) the two old men stoking the fire in the big urn in that shed. Now and then they throw white parcels into the fire. Stink of burning meat, guts, bits and pieces of people from the surgery department. (At least the sun is not ever going to change, it is forever, I hope.) On the platform outside the shed, which is what the nurses call the crematorium I think, are kerosene drums full of rubbish and flies and stink. One of the old men, the one with the billiard-bald head and the bad limp, is foraging in one of the drums. He takes out scraps and puts them into a basket. Food for his pigs, I think. He eats some of the scraps himself. Some nights a pack of dogs hangs around the urn and rubbish tins and they yelp and howl and fight over the scraps both of food and people, and I wake up in a sweat and remember the two old men and the urn and the fire and get scared.

103

The fly now lies on the window sill, legs up, still. I could have saved it, but what the hell. A fly is a fly. I must not get scared watching the two old bastards stoking their fire with the white bundles. I have no regrets. None.

There is an old woman in the next room. She is dying – so the nurse tells me – from three husbands, eighteen children and too much money. She groans and moans all night long. She begs God for her life. A pastor comes to see her every afternoon, and she weeps and he prays. But she is still going to die. No miracle to save her. Nothing. Just a scared old woman dying in a white disinfected room. I have not seen her. Perhaps like Jesus, I can command her to get up, grab her bed and go home, maggot-proof. But if the pastor cannot perform the miracle, I cannot either.

My room is getting hot, the heat is buzzing in my ears. There is a rosary hanging above my head. My wife Susana put it there last week. Now and then I get it down and count the beads and look at the silver Jesus on the silver cross, and I think the artist who made the rosary is very good. I do not understand why Susana brought it. I suppose she is still trying to save me because when I die she will not have a steady source of money. You see, like all women, Susana has based her life on safe sources of income. I was her source of money. God, she told me, is her source of 'moral and spiritual food'. Her poor faafafine halfman-half-woman father is her main source of gossip. Her poor nearly-all-male mother is her main source of thrilling punishment – apart from me. The rest of mankind, so she will tell you, is her source of 'love'. (Love for what, I do not know.) Susana by the way was and is and always will be crazy on the Roman religion. But more of that later. I have to get ready for the doctor's visit this morning.

I am a poet who is three months old. Ever since I got the Tb worm (is it a worm?) I have tried to put pen to paper to make some poetry. Before I got Tb I never had the worm for poetry. Who knows, maybe the two go together. You get Tb and you want to be a verse-maker. I grew old as a poet in three months, and I am now a poet failure. Two days ago I could not finish a three-line masterpiece, one line for every month in hospital, and so decided to become the second Robert Louis Stevenson, a tusitala or teller of tales, but with a big difference. I want to write a novel about me. By the way, here are the two lines of verse I wrote:

I am a man
Got a plan.

A novelist, so a palagi tourist once told me, has got to be honest (with whom, he did not say). So before I continue my novel let me tell you that I am, so my friends know well, a tall-teller of tales. (Or is it, a teller of tall tales?) So please read this humble testament with 15 grains of epsom salts, and please excuse the very poor grammar. You see I did not have much formal education. (Unlike many of the present generation who went away overseas and returned with degrees in such things as education, drinking, revolutions, themselves and more themselves etc. and who wave before you the rounded 'r' and the long 'e' and the short 't' in just about everything, especially their own importance.) Pepe is local-born, local-bred, local-educated, so please do not expect too much scholarship, grammar, and etc. in this weak novel about his (my) life.

The young palagi doctor came this morning as usual, and as usual I pretended I did not know any English and he pretended I was fit as a ten-ton horse. He smiled as usual, he listened to my cough as usual, and he told the nurse to give me the usual pills, as usual. While he did the usual I looked at the juicy nurse by his side. (Me, I am no longer interested in making fire.) I look at her because everytime she looks at the doctor she has the clinging octopus eye on him, but he does not know it.

Before he goes out he tells the nurse to tell me I am getting better, as usual. He smiles and winks at me as usual, then out the usual door. I pinch the nurse's juicy backside and she giggles and runs out after the doctor. 'Get him!' I call to her.

The doctor, who is a freckle-faced, blond-haired, false-toothed, rabbit-eared, woman-scared fellow of my age and who knows the female biology from books only, knows I am a goner; but because he wants to be kind to me he tells me I am recovering. He thinks like this: let him die without

105

knowing he is a hopeless case and was always a hopeless case from the day he shot out of mamma to the day he shoots back into the six-foot womb. I like this doctor, he is a gentle kid. If the nurse seduces him he will be a better man at biology and everything else. Nothing like a succulent warm hot-blooded woman to cure shyness and a nervous condition and stutters, and this doctor is a nervous condition.

I have only a few days to write this novel about the self. I was/am no hero. So if you do not like stories without heroes, you better stop reading right here. Sex, violence, plenty-action, love any style, there will be in my novel. God there will not be. No saints either. And no sermons. So straight into it without any pissing around (is that the phrase?) I cannot keep the maggots waiting.

Here we go English-style, Vaipe-style. My style.

## The Pink House in the Town

My mother Lupe is dead. My father Tauilopepe is alive. He is now one of the richest in these little islands which the big god Tagaloaalagi threw down from the heavens into the Pacific Ocean to be used by him as stepping stones across the water, but which are now used by people, like my honourable father, as shithouses, battle fields, altars of sacrifice and so on.

Like all the Tauilopepe men before me, I was born in Sapepe, and my aiga is one of the main branches of the Sapepe Family who founded the village and district of Sapepe in long ago times. Sapepe is a long way from Apia, towards the west and, so legend tells, only a short way from the edge of the world. It is one of the biggest villages in Samoa, and it is cut off from other districts by low mountains to the east and west and the main mountain range behind it. Because of these mountains, Sapepe was separated from the rest of Samoa for hundreds of years, and so Sapepe had its own history and titles and customs different in many ways from the other districts. Things did not change very much. Life was slow until the papalagi came and changed many things, including later people like my father . . . .

I get into the bus in my best clothes and sit beside Tauilopepe (Tauilo for short). I look out the bus window. Lupe, my mother, and my sisters are watching me. I look away from Lupe because I do not want to see her pain. The bus roars and off we go. I wave. My sisters call goodbye, waving to me. Lupe just stands there. I look back at her till the bus goes round the bend and I do not see her no more. Soon we pass the last fale in Sapepe and we are heading for the range eastwards to the morning sun.

The bus is full of people who laugh and talk like they are going to burn the town with their laughter. I feel hot and uncomfortable in my best clothes. Tauilo is talking with a man who has rotten teeth. Tauilo tells the man that he is going to Apia to take his son (me) to school there. The man says he wishes he had the money to send his son to a town school. Tauilo gives the man an American cigarette. They talk about the Bible and how God is good to men who work hard, and all that. It is Tauilo's usual talk. I fall asleep as we come over the range, thinking of my mother.

We get off the bus beside the Apia market and Tauilo smoothes down his clothes and leads me towards my uncle Tautala's home just behind the picture theatre. The picture theatre looks like a big tin coffin.

'Now, you behave like a man,' Tauilo tells me. 'Tautala is a God-fearing man who does not want any silly nonsense. You understand?' I nod the head. 'You work hard at school. You only going to stay with Tautala until I get enough money to buy us a house here. You understand?' I nod the head again.

I have met Tautala many times before. He used to visit Sapepe to see Lupe who is his sister, but it is only an excuse to get from us some loads of taro and bananas. Tautala is a short man who is nearly as fat as he is tall. Some of my aiga call him 'piggy' because that is what he looks like. He looks all the time like he is looking for a toilet or bit of bush to shit in. He always talks of palagi like they are his best friends. He works in a government office where he gets $12 a month. Because he is a government worker with the white shirt and shorts and long socks and shoes, just like a palagi, most of the Sapepe people, including my father,

are very impressed with him. Especially when he speaks
English, which the Sapepe people do not understand. He is
an educated man, Tauilo tells everyone. He is a palagi who
does not know how to read, some of my aiga say. A nobody
who is small between the fat legs, some of them laugh.

I look at the neighbourhood as we walk to Tautala's
house. The fale look like old men who are waiting to die.
Some of them are made of banana boxes and rusty iron,
and the area smells like a dead horse because of the toilets
on the black stream flowing through it. The stream is called
the 'Vaipe', my father tells me. (In English that means
'Dead Water'.)

We go over the small wooden bridge over the stream and
I see some children playing under the breadfruit trees, and
on the steps of a dirty-looking house there sit two women
who have on the lipstick and coloured dresses. Tauilo
sees them and he holds my hand and pulls me quickly
through the neighbourhood, and I wonder why. Then we go
through a high hibiscus hedge.

And there it is. Tautala's house. The pink house. It has
two storeys and many windows of real glass. Next to the
house is a fale with a sugar-cane patch behind it. All
around the house and fale stands a high hibiscus hedge,
just like a wall to protect something from thieves. At the
far side, over the hedge and stream, is the police station and
prison. Two boys and a girl are playing marbles in front of
the house. They come running when they see us. One boy
takes my suitcase. He is about my age but smaller. He leads
us to the door.

I have never been in a palagi home before, so when I
stand on the steps I feel like I am going to enter a temple
or something. The smell of the house and the way it is so
shiny scares me. Tauilo looks afraid too. Faafetai, Tautala's
wife, comes and welcomes us inside. (My mother told me
once that Faafetai runs Tautala's life. No wonder all the
time he looks like he is going to shit his clothes.)

'Sit down,' Faafetai says, pointing at two wooden chairs.

'It is alright down here,' says Tauilo, sitting on the shiny
floor. I sit down beside him. Faafetai sits on the chair facing
us; she smiles.

Then Tauilo and her go through the Samoan oratory of welcome.

'How is your family?' she asks later.

Tauilo is lost for words. He is in a nervous condition. 'They are well, thank you,' he says finally.

'Tautala will be home soon,' she says. She tries to smile as she looks at me and my suitcase.

'That is good. And how is he?'

'Working hard, very hard. Overtime all the time,' she says. I wonder what overtime is. 'He is so tired when he comes home that all he does is sleep.'

'Is he working on important government business?'

'Yes, all the time.'

'Did you hear that, Pepe?' Tauilo asks me. I nod the head. 'You get a good education and you will be like Tautala.' I nod again.

While they talk, I look around and sigh in wonder. There are photos of hundreds of people maybe, on the walls; smiling people, sad people, old people, ugly people, and one dead man covered with ietoga with Faafetai weeping beside him. On one wall I see certificates like the ones on our Sapepe pastor's house. All the certificates belong to Tautala. I read one. It says that Tautala passed the standard four examinations.

' . . . I will take good care of Pepe,' I hear Faafetai say.

'Thank you. He is a good boy,' says Tauilo.

At the back of the room stands a table with chairs round it. I have never eaten on a table before so I look forward to it. On the other side is the biggest radio I have ever seen. It is so shiny I want to go and touch it. Faafetai's children giggle. The girl pokes her tongue at me. I hit her. She cries. Faafetai laughs but I know she does not mean it. Tauilo tells me not to do it again or else.

'I am sorry,' he says to Faafetai.

'It is alright,' she replies.

The boy, the one who took my suitcase, comes over and sits by me. 'What is your name, boy?' he asks. I do not answer. 'Have you got a palagi house like ours?' he asks. 'Bet you do not because you are poor.' He is the most childish kid I have ever met.

'Why you come to stay here?' his sister asks. ''Cause you are poor, that is why!' She is ugly bad.

My aiga in Sapepe teach me never to let common people insult me so I say to the children, 'Who you think you are?' They sit up. I repeat what I said but they are too stupid to know what I am talking about.

'You know how to play marbles?' the boy asks.

'That game is for kids,' I reply. 'You know how to spear fish?' I ask. The children get up, poke their tongues at me and leave, and I feel good because I am alone again.

I try to remember Sapepe and how if I were there now I would be out fishing with my friends, but here I am in the pink house with only the self for company.

Then Tautala enters, panting like he is drowning, with the starched palagi clothes and long white socks and brown shoes, with pencils and pens in his shirt pocket.

'Do not get up!' he greets Tauilo. They shake hands. 'Very hot day. And how is our family?' Tauilo makes the usual reply. Tautala sinks into the soft chair next to Faafetai and is wiping his face with a red handkerchief. 'Hot day. Oh!' He gets up and nearly runs out of the room to the back. I have the feeling he is going to the toilet.

'Hot, is it not? Hungry too,' he says when he returns, wiping his hands. Faafetai goes out to get the food ready. 'Been working all day adding up government money,' he says. Then he tells Tauilo, who is sitting like a lost boy on the floor, how Dave, his palagi boss, likes him because he can add up difficult sums of money and how Dave is going to promote him soon. He takes out a silver fountain pen and shows it to Tauilo. 'Dave gave that to me last week!' Tauilo looks at the pen and sighs in envy.

I get bored. I get up and leave the house. I sit on the bank of the stream and look at the jail on the other side. Smoke is rising from the prison umu and two prisoners, in striped lavalava, are fixing the food. A fat policeman comes and talks with them. They laugh behind the barbed-wire fence.

The stream is narrow at this point, and it has a steel pipe for a bridge across it to the prison. The stream is loaded with rubbish, shit, and it stinks as I have said before. I pick up a rock and break my face in the water with it. The prisoners and the policeman are talking still. I try to hear what they are saying but they are too far away. I bend my head into my hands on my knees and cry. Even when I think of all my friends in Sapepe I am still alone. There is only the black water and the stink.

'Boy!' someone calls. I look up scared. He is a giant prisoner with a bird tattoo on his chest. 'Why you cry?' he asks. 'You got no reason to cry, you not a prisoner!' he laughs. Then he is gone into the prison.

I return to the pink house.

The next morning Tauilo takes me to enrol in the government primary school. (Tautala is a graduate of this school.) In the afternoon my father gives me $2 before he leaves on the bus for Sapepe. I stand and hold the money. He waves at me from the bus window. Then the bus is off and I am alone in the market where there are so many people buying and selling. I start to shake. It is the first time I have been alone in the town. But when I see some kids eating ice-creams I run to the shop and buy one.

I whistle and run home past the police station, eating my ice-cream.

That night my ice-cream courage leaves me as I lie in the mosquito net. I pray to God, tell Him to look after me. I fall asleep saying I am going to be alright.

## First Day School

There is no one in the classroom. A prayer comes to my mouth. I pray. Giggling behind me. I jump and look around. The two girls look queerly at me. They run away yelling, 'The new boy is a fool!'

I walk into the classroom and stand by the windows and look out at the playground. Many kids are playing out there, but they do not look real behind the dirty glass. I turn and survey the classroom.

It is a big box of cement with five windows facing the playground and rows of desks and a blackboard in front. There are pictures on the walls, and diagrams too with English sentences. I try to read a few sentences and get scared because I cannot read them very well. The classroom

111

is so different from the one in Sapepe. There, it is an open
fale and we sit on the pebble floor and it is not hot like this
one.

The slap-slap of sandals. I turn. The afakasi woman looks
at me. I at her. Then she comes in to her desk at the front
and does not look at me anymore. She is severe-looking,
like Faafetai maybe. About forty years old and going grey
in the hair already. She slaps down her satchel, papers spill
out on the desk. Her fingernails are long and red with paint.

'You the new boy?' She does not look at me.

'Yes,' I reply.

'You take the empty desk at the back.' She points to the
corner desk. She still does not look at me as she puts her
papers back into the satchel. I go and put my satchel on
the back desk. She is looking at me when I turn. 'I hear
you were in standard two?' she says in quick English.
I do not understand. 'I . . . hear . . . you . . . were . . . in . . .
standard . . . two?' she repeats slowly. I nod the head. 'I
am Mrs Brown,' she adds. I nod the head. She picks up a
chalk and starts printing on the blackboard.

'My name is Pepe,' I introduce the self. She continues to
write like she does not care whether I have a name or not.
She is skin and bone in the white shirt and black lavalava,
not in the group of female that Sapepe people call, 'Flesh-
meat for the gods'.

I look at the window because I do not know what else to
do. I see the other children playing under the tamaligi
trees, but they are so far away.

Three boys enter talking all the time and they do not see
Mrs Brown. She turns. 'You know the rule. NO NOISE.
Understand?' she says to them. The kids nod. I make up my
mind fast that I am never going to offend Mrs Brown.
Never. I sit down.

Children come in and go out. They just look at me. I at
them. But we do not say anything.

Clang-clang-clang! dongs the school bell. All the children
leave quickly. I wonder why but I sit there like a fool. She
looks at me. I at her.

'Leave. It is assembly time,' she says. I get up fast and
out to the playground.

The other children are standing in lines in front of the tamaligi trees which have a platform under them in the shade. I go and join the end of the line of the children who came into my classroom that morning. I stand at ease. Everyone is looking ahead, arms back, chests out. I do the same even though I have never been a soldier before.

'Boy, she in a bad mood today,' someone next to me says. I look round but there is no one. I look down to my left and there he is – the dwarf, the first I have ever seen. He has a shaved head and sores on it and he is only as tall as up to my biceps. Like me he wears no shirt but only a red lavalava with two white stripes on it.

'My name is Pepe,' I introduce the self.

'Mine is Tagata,' he introduces his self. He does not look at me. His eyes are looking up at the rooftops of the school. 'My father owns the market.' Then he picks his nose.

'She is going to kill someone today,' the boy next to him whispers. The speaker, who is not a dwarf, is black like midnight. He looks at me and his eyes shine like white coral in all his blackness.

'My name is Pepe,' I say to him.

He nods the head and says, 'Mrs Brown is . . . a . . . a . . . . ' But he cannot finish.

'A bitch?' I suggest. Tagata giggles but the black boy looks ahead.

'Simi's father is a pastor, that is why he does not swear,' Tagata tells me. I want to ask Tagata if Simi's parents are Solomon Islanders but I do not because it is impolite.

Clang-clang-clang! the bell rings again. Everyone is still like dead soldiers maybe. No talk.

Crunch-crunch-crunch-crunch! the shoes of the teachers march from the building toward the platform in the tamaligi shade. The sun is very hot now, it is hanging over the school like a fat boil. Crunch-crunch! the shoes stop and the teachers get on to the platform. Women in front, men behind. All in white like Sunday. I count six palagi teachers and only two Samoan. Out in front, in long socks nearly to his knees to cover his cowboy legs, is the palagi head-master.

'That is Mr Croft,' whispers Tagata. Mr Croft has short

hair the colour of the sun and white skin like cooked pork. He holds out his chest and his head up.

'Mr Croft,' Simi says, 'He used to be a captain in the army.'

'Ahh . . . ahh . . . ten-shun!' Mr Croft commands. Bang! everyone is at attention, even the teachers. 'Let us pray!' Everyone obeys. My English is not good enough to follow his fast prayer. The sun is burning my neck. Tagata is rubbing his bald head.

'NOW!' says Mr Croft, then he is off and his English is too fast for me. All I know is that he is very angry about something.

'What is he saying?' I ask Tagata.

'He is yelling that no one is allowed to go down the road at playtime because some boys stoned his house last night. He says if he catches the culprits he is going to murder them. . . . But he is never going to catch them.'

'Why not?' I ask him.

'Because I am the one who did it,' he says. That dwarf he is not afraid of anyone, not even palagi.

'Why you tell him?' whispers Simi, looking at me. 'He may tell Croft.

'You going to tell him?' Tagata asks me. I shake the head.

'Why did you do it?' I ask.

'Because he beat me last week for something I did not do,' replies Tagata. I am astounded by his bravery.

'You and Simi be my friends?' I ask. But they do not say anything.

Mr Croft finishes. He wipes the mouth with the hanky. Two boys beat drums. 'Left-turn!' shouts Mr Croft. We turn. 'Left-right, left-right, left-right!'

We march into the school building.

No one says anything as Mrs Brown takes out her books.

'Stand up!' she calls. I do not know she is calling me because she is not looking at anyone, or at me. 'Stand up!' she says again. She looks at me. I jump up. The girls giggle. 'This boy is the new boy. He is from the *back*,' she tells the others. I look at the floor at my dirty feet. 'Now he is going to give us a morning talk about his village.' She smiles for the first time. 'What is your name?' she asks.

'Pe . . . Pepe,' I stutter.

'Louder!'

'Pepe.'

'Very good. Now tell the others about your village.' She speaks slowly. I continue to look at my dirty feet. 'Come to the front!' I do not move. 'Hear me?'

My two dirty feet begin to follow one another to the front of the class. I turn. They are all looking at me.

'Well?' says Mrs Brown. I swallow tears in my throat. 'Well, go on!'

'My . . . my village . . . . '

'Louder!'

'Mine village it is called Sapepe,' I begin. Everyone laughs at my English, including Mrs Brown. I look at Simi and Tagata at the back, they are not laughing. I stop the tears and look down.

'Please, Mrs Brown,' a boy's voice saves me. I look up. It is Tagata. He has his hand up.

'Yes?' Mrs Brown asks him.

'I want to talk this morning,' says Tagata. He gets up before Mrs Brown says alright and is coming to the front to save me.

'Sit down,' she says to me. I nearly run to my desk.

Tagata stands alone. He looks everyone full in the face. No one laughs at his ugliness.

'This morning I am going to talk about the barracuda that my father bought for my mother yesterday at our market,' he begins. His English is the best I have ever heard from any dwarf or from any normal Samoan for that matter. I understand what he is saying because he speaks slowly, clearly. 'As we all know, the barracuda is a killer. It looks like a torpedo and it can torpedo through the water faster than any torpedo. And, as we all should know, torpedoes kill people!' Simi's hand is up.

'Yes?' asks Tagata.

'What is the torpedo?' Simi asks.

'Well, as we all should know, a torpedo is a bomb fired by a submarine, and when it hits something, like another ship or a whale, it goes BANG and that something is blown to bits,' he explains. But Simi's hand is up again.

'What is the whale?' Simi asks. I realise that they are playing a game like we do in Sapepe. You take a small joke and build it up till you get a deadly joke.

'Well, the whale is a mammal, the biggest mammal on earth that lives in the sea.'

'What is the mammal?'

'A mammal,' replies Tagata, 'is a big fish with a tail and a nostril and blubber and the fish which swallowed Jonah in the Bible.'

'I understand,' says Simi. I nearly burst with laughter, but no one else is laughing, they are too dumb, including Mrs Brown.

'That is my talk,' Tagata says to Mrs Brown. He comes and sits down, and Mrs Brown asks a girl to give a talk.

'Excuse me, Mrs Brown,' Tagata says. 'I want to talk about our horse.'

'What has your horse done now?' she tries to joke.

'Well, Midnight, our horse, had a child horse last night.'

'Go on,' says Mrs Brown.

'Well, Midnight never had children before,' says Tagata. Simi is laughing behind his hand. (I find out at interval from Tagata and Simi that they call Mrs Brown 'Horse' and Mrs Brown has no children either.) 'Not long ago, my father gets a stallion . . . . '

'That is enough!' says Mrs Brown. 'Sit down!' Simi's hand is up. 'Yes?' she asks him.

'What is the stallion?' Simi asks her.

'Take out your spelling books, children. Time for spelling,' she orders.

For the rest of that day she leaves Tagata and Simi and me alone.

That first day at school I also learn ten new English words: HORSE, BROWN, STALLION (Tagata teaches me what this means), BRIGHT, TOWN, SHIT (I see this on the toilet wall and Simi tells me what it means), SUN-LIGHT, SPEECH, FEMALE, and TOILET.

During the two years at primary school, I progress until I am nearly top of the class. I master the English quickly and I am always obedient to Mrs Brown, Tautala and Faafetai. Tagata and Simi and me are like brothers. Every fourth week-end and school holidays, I spend at Sapepe. But everytime I return to Sapepe, it seems like I am returning to something less important, like a step back, and I cannot help feeling this way.

At the end of these two years, Tauilo has built a large palagi house for us next to our fale in Sapepe. The house has many glass windows, five bedrooms, a big sitting room with photos on the walls, and a radio and furniture, a flush toilet which is the first and only flush toilet in Sapepe, and a room which Tauilo calls his 'office' in which he spends most of his time when he is at home, writing and writing. He buys books on bookkeeping, shorthand, and three Bibles, all in English. And a typewriter which he teaches himself to use. Tauilo also buys a safe of iron in which he locks most of his money, the rest he puts in the town bank. My father, the failed theological student who was treated by my aiga as a disgrace to the aiga because he had been expelled from Malua College, becomes the most powerful and successful son Sapepe has begotten.

In this time, the 'Leaves of the Banyan Tree', my father's plantation, covers most of the valley behind Sapepe village and is reaching out to the foothills and range, Many of the people of Sapepe now work on this plantation for wages. The money has come to stay in Sapepe.

# A Haunted House in the Town

Reader, stop here for a moment for I have to stop because the coughing is killing me. It hurts like hell. I had a short sleep this morning. When I woke up I found the self with an erection, something which surprised me because I have had no such thing for the past few weeks. I think it is because I am nearly dead. I read somewhere that when a man is hanged by the neck until dead, you find that he is hanging up there with his weapon erect like a flag waving goodbye to the hangman. I hope that when I kick the air finally they will come into my room and find my weapon laughing at them. Got to have a rest now. Am finding it hard to write longer than two hours per day.

In my fourth year at high school, Tauilo buys us a large house in Apia. The house is opposite the primary school I used to go to and it belonged to a palagi plantation owner from Germany who died at the age of eighty. He came to Samoa sixty years before. And from what I hear, he died because aitu scared him to death. He did not have a wife or children. He retired from his plantation and settled in this house all by himself. Some people will tell you that he drank himself to the grave and he used to spend his time with faafafine.

The house has many rooms and it is on stilts. It has beautiful gardens round it. Orchids, hydrangeas, bougain-viliaea, ferns, hibiscus, frangipani, flamboyant trees, tamaligi, cactus, flower of the night, puataunofo (I do not know the English for this), lilies, tiger orchids, beautiful creepers and lianas whose names I do not know. In fact just about any tropical flower you can think of.

Tauilo is not satisfied with the house. He hires carpenters and they renew it all, change it into a house like our house in Sapepe. He fills it with expensive furniture which he buys cheaply from his business friends, and he has a new toilet built. This toilet is so big you can fit maybe ten people in it. The sitting room, which takes up the whole middle and front of the house facing the road across a veranda, has a blood-coloured wall on which hang all the family photos. There is a big glass cabinet in it too. This is full of crystal glasses and bottles of whisky. (When we were poor my father was against liquor. Now he is rich he loves it, despite his deacon's position in our church; and our church preaches against alcohol, called the 'Devil's Water' by the Sapepe people.) Beside the cabinet is a long three-shelf bookcase where Tauilo keeps books he buys but does not read. Behind the house Tauilo builds a fale in which some of my Sapepe aiga come to stay to serve us, the people in the house.

Tauilo comes to spend nearly all his week-ends in this house. He puts on parties for his town friends. I never once see a Samoan at these parties. Only palagi and rich afakasi etc. Even my aiga are not allowed to attend as guests. He is ashamed of his relatives, they are good only as servants to his guests. When I shift into this house away from the Tautalas I am barman at these parties, but I am not allowed to touch a drop of the Devil's Water. Lupe, my mother, shifts here too. Tauilo says that the town climate will be good for her failing health.

Lupe is very interested in the old German who owned the house before us. When anybody in Apia visits her she always asks them if they knew the German and how he died, whether he died of aitu or not. Everyone tells her that he died because of loneliness and drink, but she does not believe them. When she is alone in the house she goes through it looking into every corner, but she does not find any trace of the man who lived there before. Tauilo tries to get members of our aiga to change the flower gardens into taro patches but Lupe will not allow it. It is in these gardens that she spends her evenings before the sun sets completely. She wanders through them like a bird looking for a nest which it can never find. If it is dark, she never goes near the gardens because she believes that when it is darkness the gardens belong again to the German whose aitu she thinks is wandering the world because he was not accepted into heaven.

## Into the Dead Water

And so I begin my journey into the Vaipe neighbourhood, into what churchgoers call the dark world of sin and allthings that they believe is against religion and good living. For some years I still live with Lupe and never visit Sapepe because Tauilo does not allow me. (He says I am a disgrace to the aiga because I got expelled from school.) And because Sapepe holds little for me now. During this time I do not need to work because Lupe gives me all the money I need. Anyway, I only sleep and eat at home, the rest of the time I journey out into Apia and the Vaipe.

Tagata, who left high school three years before me, hears that I have been expelled and he laughs like it is the funniest joke he ever heard. I laugh with him. For months Tagata and me form our own team.

The market, which is owned by Tagata's parents, sprawls

over a big area. It smells of rotting food and people and is loud all the time with people's conversation and buying and cheating, but I soon get used to it. Tagata and me go to the movies about every night. The cowboy movies are the best because they have the action and blood and quick justice. Tagata and me wear jeans like the cowboy. We smoke the American cigarettes, drink the yankee coca-cola, and talk smooth like the gangsters of Chicago. We can smooth-talk any stranger to make the easy dollar and laughter. . . .

Late Sunday night. Apia is quiet like the graveyard. I suddenly feel we are aitu that are going to haunt Apia for a long time. And I feel invisible and powerful. Tagata and me are in command of the operation, so the movies say. There are twelve of us behind the store. Twelve disciples. In the dark. Just like in the movies, but this is not make-believe, and I shake like the breeze blowing through Apia.

The town clock strikes the midnight hour when Sapepe people believe the aitu come out of their graves to haunt the living. There is nobody in the streets. Only a few street lights are on. Now.

'Got the kerosene?' I whisper to the boy who is in charge of the fire.

'What building?' he asks.

'Any one on the other side of town,' I reply without thinking smart enough. 'Start the fire in one half hour. Make sure it is big.' The five boys move off into the streets.

There are seven of us left. I instruct two to go and hide on the other side of the store and watch out for the police just in case they come too early. There are five left, and Tagata is breathing heavy beside me.

The silence is dead as we wait for the sound of the fire engine and siren. My throat is dry sand. There are stars in the sky. Tomorrow will be fine.

The fire siren wails like madness. One boy runs and tells me that the fire is in full swing. It is the Protestant Church Hall that is being eaten by the flames. I do not care.

We smash open the glass doors and rush in with torches. The others fill their baskets with food and clothes and other goods. Tagata and me run upstairs and smash into the office. I break open the drawers and small safe. We fill the bag with money. Then move down and out the front door.

The police car lights hit us for a moment as we dive over the road and then sprint along the waterfront in the shadows.

'Stop!' they shout. We keep running past the wharf. Tagata is too slow, they will catch us. I stop.

'Some bastard told the cops!' he says to me. I give him the bag of money.

'You go on ahead!' I tell him. He does not want to. I push him forward. He disappears. I rip off my shirt and dive behind the wooden fence.

I hear one cop coming past fast. I whip behind him, smash down on his neck with the open hand like the detective in the movies, and he goes down without a sound. I turn and run off towards Mulinuu to lead them away from Tagata. The shadows hide me.

I hear them behind me. I dive behind the tree in front of the Crown Estates building. The footsteps come. I step out. He is too slow. I kick up and get him in the balls. He groans and goes down. I kick him again in the gut to make sure he stays down.

They are still coming. The street light catches me. I break through the hibiscus hedge in front of the Casino Hotel. I duck too late. The night watchman sees me plain as sunlight. I leave him alone even though he is sure to recognise me.

I look back. The police are in front of the Crown Estates. I run along behind the hedge and into the dark again and cross back over the road and jump on to the beach and into the sea. The cold hits me, gives me back my breath. I swim quietly towards the buoy in the middle of the harbour. Well out, I float and look back at the shore. The police lights go past the Casino, heading for Mulinuu. I am safe.

The buoy rises up and down under me. My teeth chatter. The lights of the town are all on. At one end the church hall is burning quickly to the ground, with a large crowd and helpless firemen watching it. The wind hits me with the cold, and the stars are laughing in the sky. Fear freezes me when I remember the night watchman.

I wait until the Protestant Hall collapses and the flames start to die out. My bones are stiff and hurting. I dive into the sea and start for the market.

121

Tagata opens the door of his home when I knock. I fall into his arms. He sits me down and gets me a towel. 'They catch no one,' he says. 'But the police will be coming here for sure. They always do.'

He supports me as we hurry to my home. We keep in the shadows. 'Just like in the movies,' he says to cheer me up. I nod the head.

'We beat them,' I whisper.

The next morning I do not leave our house. That afternoon, Tauilo storms into the house. I hear him cursing the people who robbed *his* store. I get dressed and go to him in the sitting room. He is reading his account books. He looks up at me and then back into his accounts.

'What you grinning at?' he asks me. I say nothing, just watch him. He is flabby now, and has grey in his hair. We are the same height and I am catching up to him in strength. He has five stores in Sapepe and other villages, twelve buses, also shares in many town businesses. Also two palagi houses, six trucks, about six hundred acres of the best cocoa plantation, plenty in the bank, a lawyer, and the whole of Sapepe under his command. I nearly laugh when the thought comes to me that I am his only heir now. Me, the worthless and only son. He looks ridiculous with his spectacles half way down his nose. He does not need glasses really. He looks like he is preparing a sermon.

Lupe enters and sits down. I look at her from across the room where I am sitting and notice that life seems to be returning to her as she watches Tauilo, knowing he has been robbed. And I believe then that she hates him in some ways.

'About $1000 in damage and goods and money!' he says and stands up.

'What happened?' Lupe asks him as if she does not know already.

'Get me a whisky,' he says to her. She does not move. I get one for him.

Lupe leaves and goes into the gardens outside. I watch her from the window. She starts planting flowers. It is the first time I have seen her doing this.

I get Tauilo another whisky and then leave for the market. Three policemen are talking with Tauilo when I return

122

home in the evening. I feel no fear. I sit down. I know all the policemen. One of them is Galo, the sergeant I knew from the time I stayed with Tautala. Tauilo is very angry about something with the police. I wait for it. The police do not look at me.

'You do it, boy?' Tauilo asks me. I look puzzled. 'Did you rob *our* store?' I shake the head. 'See, my son says he did not do it,' Tauilo says to the police. 'And my son does not tell me lies!' The police look at each other, they are afraid of Tauilo.

'The night watchman at the Casino tells us that it was your son who did it, sir,' Galo says softly to Tauilo.

'You believe him or me?' Tauilo warns. Galo looks at the floor. 'Pepe is not a liar. He is my flesh and blood!'

'They have to do their job,' I tell Tauilo. 'Ask me any question,' I tell Galo.

'Go on,' Tauilo says to him. 'Ask him anything. He will tell you he did not do it.'

Galo clears his throat and asks me, 'Where were you last night?'

'Sleeping in my room,' I say.

'You prove that?'

I look at Tauilo and suddenly want him to lie for me. 'Ask my father,' I tell Galo. There is silence.

'Yes, he was sleeping here,' Tauilo says.

'Did you see him, sir?' Galo asks.

'Of course I saw him. You do not take my word for it?'

And immediately the police are lost. Tauilo tries not to look at me. I burst out laughing and the police are puzzled.

'I did it,' I tell them. They look scared. Tauilo has his back to me. 'I did it alone.'

'You sure?' Galo asks.

'I am sure,' I reply. I stand up. 'We go now?' I walk to the front door.

'He tells you a lie!' Tauilo shouts to the police.

I stop and face him. 'My father is the liar,' I say and then walk out.

The police follow me.

Tauilo slams the door behind us.

# Trial of the Native Son

Galo brings to my cell a breakfast of butter and jam and bread and tea. He sits down opposite me while I eat.

'You know something?' he says.

'What?' The bread and tea tastes good for I have not eaten for a day.

He looks away from me and says, 'You can be free.'

'Can I have some more tea?' I ask. He pours me another.

'They are calling it the 'Big Robbery' already.'

'Who?'

'Everyone, even my sons. You are a hero. They are going to make songs and stories about you. But me, I am going to be the villain in them. I do not mind though because I am doing my job.'

'How long you been a police?' I ask.

'Twenty years.'

'Long time. Good job?'

'It is a job someone has to do,' he says.

We do not say anything for a while.

'You can be free,' he says.

'How?' I extend the empty cup. He fills it.

'The night watchman has no proof you are guilty. It is only his word.'

'But he tells the truth.'

'It is his word against yours,' he says. I hand him the empty cup and plate.

'Who you afraid of?' I ask. 'Is it my father?'

He gives me a cigarette. 'Pepe, I have known you for a long time. You got everything. Money, brains, a future. Me, I got nine children and a big aiga. I struggled to get where I am.'

'Galo, I am not changing my mind.'

'You sure?' he asks. I nod the head. 'Anything else you need?' I shake the head. 'Do not blame me, Pepe.'

'For what?'

'For what I will have to do against you.'

'It is your job,' I reply.

'Yes, it is my job,' he says. Then he leaves.

After noontime, when my cell is hot, they come and take

me to the office for questioning. 'Who you taking the blame
for? Who else did it with you?' They keep asking. But I
stick to my story. They keep on for hours until they are
sweating and their uniforms are soaked. Galo leads all the
questions, he does his job well.

'I also hit those police and I burned the hall down,' I add.
I notice they are not writing anything down for evidence.

'If we charge you with robbery, arson and assault,' says
Galo, 'the Judge is going to send you to prison for a
long time.'

But I do not budge.

The palagi Commissioner enters and sits down beside
Galo. He smokes and watches me, the others continue
their questioning. The Commissioner, so the Vaipe people
have told me, is a cruel man. There are stories of Mr Towers
(that is his name), about how he likes to watch people
suffer. (His wife, after one year in Samoa, leaves him and
returns to New Zealand.)

Towers goes with many women, especially after he watches
somebody suffering. A few years before, three men escape
from Tafaigata prison and one of them puts a rifle bullet
in Towers's lung. They say the bullet is still there and is
poisoning him slowly.

'Why you telling all these lies, boy?' Towers suddenly
asks me in English. 'You never did it alone.' Galo starts
to interpret into Samoan.

'You scared of my father too?' I ask him in English.
Towers jumps up.

'Boy, your father is a good man. I do not know how he
comes to have so bad a son like you,' he says. I do not reply,
I stare back at him. 'You believe in religion, boy?'

'It does not interest me,' I say.

'You love your mother, boy?' He is smiling now. I am
suspicious about his questions because they have nothing
to do with my crimes. 'You love her?' he repeats.

'Yes,' I say.

'You lie, you are never home, you do not look after her.
You are destroying her slowly. Am I right?' I do not reply.
I notice Galo is now writing down everything. I am puzzled
by this.

'If you are a Christian, why you burn down the Church Hall?' Towers asks next.

'Because God does not live in it, and I do not want to burn places in which people live,' I reply.

'You an atheist?' Towers is like the preacher on the pulpit, like Tauilo.

'What is atheist?' I ask.

'He is an atheist,' Towers says to Galo. 'Put that down.' Galo writes it in the book. The other police look at me in a strange way as if I have a aitu inside me. 'Bring the Bible,' Towers instructs them.

When the Black Book comes, Towers holds it out to me and says, 'Take it.' I smile and take it. 'You ready to swear you alone committed the robbery, arson and assault, boy?' I nod the head. It is all ridiculous. The other police look afraid, perhaps they are waiting for their God to strike me dead if I lie on the Black Book.

'Say it!' Towers says.

'I swear by your almighty God and your almighty Book that I robbed your store and bashed your police. Alright?' I swear. While I say it, Galo is looking up like he is expecting the holy thunderbolt to burn me to cinders like the church hall.

'And you burned God's Hall,' Towers adds.

'And I burned your hall to ashes,' I say.

'Put that all down. Every word of it,' Towers instructs Galo.

'What does all that prove?' I ask. Towers smiles.

'You will find out. Wait till you appear before *him*.'

'Him?'

'The Judge. He is going to put you away for a very long time of hard labour!' He laughs for the first time. Some of the police join him as if the joke is on me now. It has something to do with the Judge, but I do not understand as yet.

That evening before the sun is fully set Galo brings Lupe to my cell. I turn away from her who is no longer the Lupe I once knew. She stands and cries.

'Stop crying,' I tell her.

'Pepe, you tell them you did not do it, please!' she pleads.

I sit her down on the cell bed. I stand looking out the window at the blood-red west where Sapepe is and always will be, at where the alive Lupe I loved is buried. And I can never forgive Tauilo for that. 'Pepe, please tell them what they want. You the only thing I have left!'

'It is too late,' I tell her. I do not know what else to say.

'It is not. They told me that if you confess they will set you free!'

'You do not understand,' I say. 'Not anymore.'

'But I do, Pepe!'

'We are both different people now.'

'Tell them everything, Pepe. I understand, you just do not want to tell on your friends. That is what Tauilo told me!'

And I know then that they and Tauilo are using her again. 'So it is for Tauilo you are doing this?' I turn to face her.

'No, Pepe. It is for me, your mother!'

'You do not remember anymore what he did to you and what he is doing to you now!'

'He loves me, Pepe. He loves you too still,' she cries. And I have to look away from the death and suffering I see in the woman who gave me birth and life.

'You better leave. It is late, too late,' I tell her. She is weeping again and I want to shut my ears and heart to her, to the beautiful memory of her back there in Sapepe in the years of my childhood before Tauilo destroyed it all. 'Galo!' I call.

He enters and looks at her and then at me and I see dislike in his eyes for me. 'Take her out,' I tell him. I turn to the window. The sun has drowned in Sapepe, the edge of the world.

Her footsteps fade away from my life.

The court room is like the inside of the Sapepe church. On my left is the high pulpit in which the Judge will sit in his throne. On the wall behind him is a picture of the New Zealand and Samoan flags. I am sitting in front of the pulpit with my back to the windows that look out on to the main street and harbour. Opposite me at a desk sits the prosecutor in his police uniform. To his right is a wooden cage with a bench inside it. This is where the accused usually sits but seeing I am defending myself I do not have to sit in it. The congregation has been coming in all the time and sitting on the rows of benches that extend right to the back, all facing the pulpit. Soon the court is full and the congregation is looking at me. The Judge is late. Two reporters come in and sit near the Prosecutor; they look at me, their eyes say nothing, all they want is news. Some of the congregation are talking, and I know they are talking about me, making up stories they will return with to the villages and tell the others. Most of my Vaipe friends are in the congregation.

'Stand!' commands the policeman who enters and stands in front of the pulpit. The police behind me tell me to stand. Silence. No one moves.

The door behind the pulpit to the right opens. The Judge enters. He looks like a priest in his black silk dress and white wig and shiny black shoes and steel spectacles. My Judge, my priest, my confessor. He looks at no one. The sound of his shoes tap across my heart and up into the pulpit and throne.

The congregation bow their heads. The Black-dress, my Judge, is praying. I begin to understand with fear why the Commissioner and police asked me about religion and God.

They tell me to stand up again.

One police in a loud voice reads out the crimes I committed. The congregation sighs in wonder.

'You plead guilty, or not?' the police asks.

'Guilty,' I reply. The congregation talks in surprise because I am not fighting. The reporters are writing.

The Black-dress wants to speak. It wants to know. 'Bring him forward,' It orders. The police take me up to stand in front of the pulpit.

My fear begins but I want to know who the Black-dress is. I look up at the face. It is pale behind glass, and the mouth is thin, the eyes are deep under the forehead and they show nothing – like the eyes of the owl that was the Tauilopepe Family god in ancient times. The head is with a wig. The rest is black like wet river stone. It is a face you can see everywhere but you do not take much notice of it because it is the face of everybody you do not really remember. It is not important whether the face is white or black or brown or yellow.

The Black-dress is going to speak.

'What is your name?' It asks in English of me. The interpreter starts to interpret. I silence him. The eyes of the Black-dress burn for a moment, then go dead. I will play my joke.

'My name is Pepesa, son of Sapepe and the gods of Sapepe,' I declare in Samoan. The congregation talk in surprise. They know I am fighting at last, putting on a good show like in the movies.

'Pepesa? Why Pepesa?' It asks in Samoan.

'After the Sapepe hero who challenged all the gods and won,' I reply. But It does not smile or is amused.

'Good. But why "son of the gods"?' It asks.

'Because it is my genealogy.' I am feeling relaxed and want to tell It everything because It is taking my joke seriously.

'To the gods?' It asks.

'Yes, to the gods.'

'In our century as well?'

'Yes, in our century,' I extend the joke. It thinks for a moment.

'This is the Twentieth Century. There is one God.' It looks at me dead-on down. It is not a joke to him and It does not know who I am yet. 'You know who the missionaries were?'

'Yes, I know.'

'Who?'

'They break through the skies of our world and bring guns and the new religion and the new God and drive my gods into the bush and mountains where they live today,' I declare, nearly laughing. Some of the congregation talk loudly. The Black-dress raps the hammer down.

'The missionaries brought you the Light!' The voice is hard like the steel of Its spectacles. I hear the silence round me and in me.

'It is not for me to say whether the missionary brought the Light as you call it,' I reply. The right arm of the Black-dress rises up like the wing of a black bird. It starts to recognise who I am.

129

'Why not?' It demands.

'Because they are dead and gone and I am still here. We are still here,' I say. Some of the congregation talk again. The hammer goes Bang-bang-bang! Silence again. It coughs, picks up the glass and drinks the medicine.

'I cannot believe you,' It says after It wipes the mouth. 'Are you a Christian?' And now I understand why the police asked me all those questions and my courage to joke begins to go. 'Are you a Christian?' It repeats.

I remember a trial scene in one American gangster movie, and reply, 'I do not want to answer that in case I will incriminate myself!' Some of the people laugh. It silences them with the hammer.

'Now, boy, if you are not serious, I will punish you severely. Understand?' It says. The Black-dress has no sense of humour – like all other preachers and gods, the modern-type. But I cannot go back on my challenge. I am committed to Pepesa. 'I repeat, boy, ARE YOU A CHRISTIAN?' Everyone waits for my answer.

'I do not know because I do not know what a Christian is,' I hear the self saying aloud.

'You go to church?'

'One time I did,' I reply. It says nothing to that.

'Why you burn down the Hall of God?' It asks me slowly.

'To take the police away from the store I was robbing.'

'Do not lie, boy. You have said already you are a pagan, a heathen!' It stops, then says, 'I ask you again: do you believe in Jehovah?' I shake the head. 'Speak up!'

'No!' I reply. The congregation is in an uproar, most of them are against me now. The Black-dress makes them quiet.

'Why you not believe in *our* God?' It asks next.

'You will not understand,' I say.

'Answer now!' It commands. Suddenly I get the feeling It is afraid of me.

'Because I know there is none.'

'How?' It says quickly.

'Because of who and what I am.'

'And what is that?' It looks amused.

'You were the one who told me who I am,' I reply, looking straight into the steel spectacles.

'A pagan?' It is smiling. I bow the head. 'Then you live in darkness and have nothing.'

I look up and say, 'I have the darkness and my self.'

It sighs for me and what It is going to do to me. 'No wonder you took to crime. You are evil. You are sick.' It stops for a moment. 'Do you think there is something or someone like God?' It asks. It is still not satisfied.

I nod the head slowly. I know what Its next question will be and I feel I no longer have the courage to answer it honestly because they will not understand and never will.

'What is it then?' It leans forward. I hear It breathing. 'Go on.'

'I have only my darkness and my self living in my world, therefore . . . . ' I stop.

'Therefore, what?'

I look straight into Its face. 'Therefore I am my god.' It blinks; the congregation is stunned. The criminal is mad, they now think. A few people laugh.

'Now I know why you committed all those evil things. You are a victim of your own madness. The Devil has led you astray.' It stops. 'That is why I am going to be lenient – yes, lenient – on you. Your father is a good man. Perhaps you will become like him after we train you in jail to join us again. You were the ideal son who fell by the wayside, a prodigal son. No human being can be God, boy. There is only one God . . . . ' As it talks on and on I think I am listening again to my father Tauilo, to all preachers in their wooden thrones who do not listen to their own message because their hearts are stone. 'We will pray for your repentance, for the healing of your madness by our Loving Father,' It ends Its sermon. 'You got anything to say, Pepe?' It asks. It is the first time It has called me by my name.

What is the use? The world now is their world and they will not understand anything I say. So I shake the head. I turn and face the congregation. Apart from my friends, they all look at me with their silence as if I am the aitu the missionaries banished. There is a world between us, I feel.

131

A sky of stone, a river of stone, a silence as deep as the grave door, between them and me and people like me. I can do nothing to change that. Nothing.

The police make me take my seat.

The Black-dress stands up. We stand and wait for It to leave the throne. Down the steps It comes. It suddenly stumbles to Its knees, the wig falls off Its head. Black human hair. The Black-dress is human after all, naked without his wig of power. He looks at me, grabs his wig, puts it on, and hurries out the door with my smile chasing him.

I get four years hard labour.

## Lava

' . . . This world that people believe they want so much is only true in the movies because people make the movies. You get me?' says Tagata. I shake the head. 'Okay, well let me explain it this way,' he continues. 'Have you seen the lava fields in Savaii?' I shake the head again. 'Two years ago I went there with some friends. You travel for miles through forest and so many villages where the people have ruined the beauty, and then . . . . And then It is there. You feel you are right in it at last. Get me? Like you are there where the peace lies, where all the dirty little places and lies and monuments we make to our selves mean nothing because lava can be nothing else but lava. You get me?' He stops for a while and looks at me. 'The lava spreads for miles right into the sea. Nothing else. Just black silence like the moon maybe. You remember that movie us guys saw years ago? Well, it looks like that, like the moon surface in that movie. A flood of lava everywhere. But in some places you see small plants growing through the cracks in the lava, like funny stories breaking through your stony mind. Get me? I felt like I have been searching for that all my miserable life. Boy, it made me see things so clear for once. That being a dwarf or a giant or a saint does not mean anything.' Tagata's eyes glow brightly. 'That we are all equal in silence, in the nothing, in lava. I did not want to leave the lava fields, but . . . but then you cannot stay there forever because you will die of thirst and hunger if you stay. There is no water, no food, just lava. All is lava.'

132

## Wife and Son

As I am drinking faamafu with Tagata and other friends in the fale on the other side of the picture theatre, Susana enters. She is the daughter of the man who owns the fale and the faamafu that costs 20 sene a bottle. She is younger than me but she is the best-looker I have ever seen. She has graduated from the Sisters' school and is a typist for the government. As she goes behind the curtains on the opposite side of the fale, she stops and looks quickly at me before she disappears. All my friends are after her, but her parents make sure no one gets near her.

We drink some more. Some of the men start talking sexy about Susana. I am getting angry about that. 'Bet you she be terrific in bed!' laughs someone. 'She is virgin for sure!' They laugh again.

All around the lights of the other fale and shacks are on and there are people moving about preparing the food and bathing and getting ready for sleep. Susana comes out of the curtains. The other men stop talking and look at her. She is frightened and walks quickly out to the back fale where her family are having their evening meal.

I drink until the head turns round and round and I cannot sit properly. Tagata and others hold me up and take me home and put me to bed. All the time, I am mumbling to Tagata that I sure want to be with Susana. He says he will fix it for me. Before this, after I leave our home for good, I am never attracted like this to any female. For me there is no shortage of women at the market. They come from everywhere. Village women, nurses, wives, half-virgins, fun women, unsatisfied women, women who go willing for money, plain women, pretty women, cat women, old women, cold women, ugly women, tourist women who look for the polynesian noble savage with the mighty club, but no one like Susana.

The next night Tagata disappears from our home. He returns laughing and tells me what happened.

He walks right into the fale and sees Susana's father. Tagata sits on the floor and faces him. Tagata buys some faamafu and they drink and talk about religion and everything. Now Tagata, as you know, is a professional gunfighter at conversation. He can talk on the Bible and dazzle anyone, which is what he did to Susana's father. In the middle of their talk Susana enters and irons clothes not far from Tagata who knows she is listening to everything he is saying. Before Tagata ends his talk he asks the man (and Susana) that they, because they are devout Christians, should pray to Jehovah to forgive him because he has been a sinner all his life. The man, who wants favours from Tagata because he owns the market, prays for Tagata who bows his head but from the corner of his eyes he sees Susana praying too. After the long prayer, Tagata asks Susana questions about her religion. He tells her he is interested because he wants to join the 'true church'. Susana, with her father's permission, at once goes into a long talk about her faith. Her father starts to fall asleep. Tagata tells him politely to go to bed. Because he still does not trust Tagata the man goes to sleep behind the curtains. From there he can hear if Tagata tries anything with Susana. Tagata soon hears him snoring so he tells Susana that he has a best friend who is keen on joining her faith too. Susana asks who it is. He tells her that it is Pepe who told the Judge that there is no God. She falls for that. When you going to talk to Pepe? he asks her. It has to be soon, he tells her, because Pepe is low in sin and there is nobody to help him see the Light. She says very soon. But what about her father? he asks. She will fix that, she says.

Tagata ends his story and we are laughing. As I said before, Tagata is a great storyteller and I do not know whether the whole story is all true or not, but I believe him.

The next night I dress up respectable and go to the fale. They sit me down. Susana's mother is there too. I get the feeling they do not only want me to be a Roman follower but also a husband for Susana. (They know that Tauilo is a rich man and I am his only son.) They talk all the time about religion. Susana's parents I mean. Susana sits and looks everywhere but at me. I get bored with their talk but I look interested in it.

Near midnight I leave.

For four nights or so the same thing happens when I visit them. I get angry because the plan is not working. It is soon Vaipe talk that I am after Susana as my permanent wife. Susana's father spreads this rumour. Her mother, who is more man than female, starts to visit the market, which I am helping Tagata's parents run, and act there like she owns me already. My friends laugh at me. I want to give up this stupid courting, but everytime I try to I remember Susana more alive than before. It is like the attraction of some people to religion, the sinner to his confessor and forgiver, the miser to his money. She is like the Hollywood dream. It is a new madness for me.

On the seventh night I run through the rain to her home and am surprised because she is by herself. Her parents are ready for sleep behind the curtains and the rest of their aiga are in the back fale. She does not look at me. She watches the rain.

She starts talking the usual about religion but her voice is unsure. I watch her closely. I let her talk on. I find myself moving over slowly till my knee is against her knee. She jumps away a bit, but she remains next to me. Her lips quiver and, even when it is chilly, she looks hot.

Now as you know, fale are open on all sides and everyone can see inside when the light is on. People run by in the rain. It is impossible for me to win her right there where every shadow can see us. As she talks my right hand falls to lie on her knee. She pretends my hand is not there. 'Now, Pepe, God is good to all men,' she is saying. My hand slides down to her thigh. She talks faster. Her parents will not hear because of the rain. 'He will be good to you if you repent. . . . ' My hand slides down her lap. She is shivering a bit. 'God is everyone's Father, and He loves you and me. . . . ' The hand caresses down there and discovers soft hair, and the fingers are alive and they play slowly. 'Now if you are a sinner and you want to be with God you got to be good and repent now. . . . ' Her legs move apart a little bit and her lavalava opens more and I see the black down there which is a small forest where the fingers are searching for the stream, and my heart beats in my ears and eyes and head. Her voice chatters like she is cold but she keeps talking.

135

I find the stream. The fingers caress. The stream flows. 'Pepe . . . God . . . God is love . . . God, ohhh!' Her eyes are shut tight.

'Susana!' her mother calls. Susana pushes my hand away and jumps to her feet. 'Go to bed!' her mother says. She moves to leave. I whisper to her that I will come and see her when the light is out. She says nothing. She goes over and switches out the light and I hear her running down the back steps into the rain and then into the back fale which has no light on now. I creep after her.

I stand outside and can see little into the back fale. My eyes get used to the darkness. I am nearly soaking wet. I now see figures of people sleeping, but not Susana. However, I soon see someone waving to me from the far side. It is her. I enter. All the people are asleep, some are snoring. One step, two steps. Someone in front of me moves. I stop dead. If they catch me they will kill me alive. The person is still again. I step over him. One step, two steps and over the next person. It is the longest walk I ever made. I step over the fourth person. And then Susana is there lying under the sheet.

I lie down beside her. She lies still and does nothing. I move close to her till I am against her warm side. All the while my ears are wide open. They will kill me for sure. I caress her hair and slowly pull down the sheet off her. My hand falls to her breasts, she draws the deep breath. I pull up her shirt till it is round her shoulders and my fingers play tunes on her breasts and belly. Her skin is smooth like sleep.

'No, Pepe. It is a sin!' she whispers. But she does not stop my cheeky fingers that have reached the top of her lavalava and are undoing it. 'Please, Pepe. It is a sin!' The lavalava is now down by her sides, the fingers are caressing her thighs and soon find the forest again. She does not move at all and she has her arm across her face. I kiss her face and body and then lie on her and she moves her legs apart. 'It is a sin, sin!' she whispers. I kneel between her legs. I shed my human clothes.

And then kneel down on she. The barrier is there in her sea. She starts to cry. Her virgin-ness is strong. I try slow.

136

No show. All the while her sound is complaining it is a sin.

Hard. Success at last. She folds up in pain. I embrace her and move slowly in her sea, and she is responding like a woman should. Every trick I try to make her come but I find the self too eager and I am giving her the seed and the fire explodes in my eyes.

She flings her arms round me. 'Pepe, I love you,' she says. That hits me in the gut. I am not in love with her, and I know she does not feel that about me. 'It is a sin what we did,' she says. 'But it is not a sin if we get married in the church. That is what my mother said.'

I put on my clothes and creep out of the fale. I am never going to see her again. The whole dream is a fake, hollow. They planned it all.


For a few months Tagata's parents go to American Samoa for holidays and Tagata and me are left to manage the market. I slowly notice that something is happening to Tagata, he looks sick but he never tells me the trouble, he does not do his job properly so I do all the work and the market makes more money than before. I introduce new methods and keep account books. Some people tell that my success is because I am Tauilo's son and business runs in my aiga's blood.

Tagata starts to stay in his room most of the time and he grows his hair long. Sometimes he does weightlifting and goes for long runs to get fit. To cheer him up I join his exercises. He is escaping I think, and it is like a new madness. He is like the flying-fox, which is his nickname, that has no nest with other birds because they laugh at him and treat him different because he is not what a bird should be. Now he, my brother, is trying to grow and be like other men, that is my understanding of his problem. Why he suddenly starts to do this, I never find out.

Because of the hard work at the market and my worries about Tagata, I forget Susana.

Tagata suddenly takes up the L.M.S. religion. I am really worried because it is against what he believed before. Every Sunday he puts on his white clothes and goes to church.

However, when he returns and I see he is happy, my worry goes away. It is at this time that Susana comes into my life again.

In the small market office, I am working on the books. There is a knock on the door. I open it. It is Susana's father.

'Have you come?' I greet him.

He stands looking at the floor and says, 'Yes, sir.' When he calls me sir I get suspicious at once. Most people in the market when they want something for free start to flatter you.

'Sit down!' I give him a chair.

'No thank you, sir.' He stands there. I know him very well, he has a reputation for making the last penny off his starving mother.

'What you want?' I ask him straight.

Then his wife fills the doorway. Susana does not look like both of them put together. The mother is like the cow, and the father is small like a sick pig.

She sits in the chair without asking me and says, 'Hot day, is it not?' I stare straight at her. 'How is the business, Pepe?' Then she laughs. I do not reply. She scratches the armpits. Her husband is still looking at the floor. 'You not been for a long time to see us,' she says. 'We still have the best faamafu. For you, it is free!' She roars the laughter again.

'I have much work to do,' I tell them.

'You go ahead,' she says, winking at me. 'Boy, you really educated and brainy as your father. Look at all those figures and books you are adding up. You wrote all those?' I do not answer. She picks up one book and looks at it. 'Pepe is bright,' she says to her husband. 'Look at all this English and figures. He is as bright as any palagi. You making much money these days?' she asks. 'Business is bad for us. We find it hard to feed all our big aiga.'

'What you want?' I ask. She looks at her husband, he is still looking at the floor. She coughs but he still does not do anything. 'What is it?' I ask him.

He blinks and whispers, 'It . . . it is our Susana, sir.'

138

'Louder!' she commands him.

'It is about Susana, sir,' he repeats. She nods.

'What about her?' I ask. She is looking at me like I am the fly and she is the spider.

'She is . . . she is with child, sir,' he says, and he looks at me for the first time that day.

'What that got to do with me?' I demand. He does not say anything.

'Tell him,' she orders him.

He blinks again and says, 'Susana says . . . . ' And stops. Blinks and says, 'She says you are the father, sir.'

'Now we are not saying that you are the father, Pepe. Susana is saying it,' she says.

'You trying to blackmail me?' I ask.

'No, but Susana said . . . . ' she says.

'Said what?' I demand.

'Tell him!' she orders him. He shakes the head. 'Tell him what your daughter said. Go on!'

'She may be lying,' I say.

'Oh, Pepe, she does not lie to me. Oh, no. She is a religious girl,' she says.

'Yes, Susana is a good girl,' he says. 'She is not like the other girls in the Vaipe.'

'If she is so good,' I say, 'why she got the fat belly now?' I have them. She sits and he stands, they are both looking at the floor.

I sit and look out at the people passing by and I remember Sapepe and my mother Lupe and my anger goes. The desire for someone of my own flesh to care for and give meaning to me fills me as I watch the market people. My own child growing in Susana's womb, the meaning perhaps to all the gone years. A son or a daughter.

Tagata bursts into the room. 'It is all a lie!' he laughs. 'I am sick of religion!' It is the same Tagata again and I am full of joy. He stops his dancing when he sees Susana's parents. He looks at them and then at me. 'What is the matter?' he asks me.

'Susana is going to have my child,' I tell him. He jumps up and down, then he runs out into the market. I hear him telling our friends that he is going to be an uncle.

'I will take her as my wife, but I do not want you to come near me and my family, understand?' I threaten Susana's parents.

'Yes, sir,' he says. She gets up angrily and leaves.

So it passes that Susana comes to stay with me in Tagata's home which is now my home too. She insists we get married in church. I refuse absolutely.

## Last Will and Testament of the Flying-fox

. . . One morning I wake to find Tagata gone. I send friends to look for him. They cannot find him anywhere. Even the police and the hospital do not know where he is.

I wait for him for six days. On the seventh, he returns. His hair and beard are long and uncombed and his clothes are torn and dirty and his eyes glow like those of the prophets in the desert.

'I went back, Pepe. Back to the lava fields, and it has brought me up from hell again. Lava is the only true thing left. It cannot change. The rock from whom we came, and it is with us at the back of our souls. You get me?' he says. 'It is there I found the self again. And the courage to accept all that has happened!' He laughs then and he seems his usual self again and I believe he is going to be okay. So I leave for work in the market.

That evening, when the sun sets over the sea and the birds fly back to the mountains and the forests, and the market is empty and shut down, I return home.

I find him hanging down from the mango tree behind the house.

I cut him down and take him into the house.

I bathe him.

I dress him.

I find this letter in English on my table:

140

*The Vaipe,*
*Judgement Day.*

*To His Excellency,*
*Pepesa Tauilopepe,*
*Illegitimate Son of the Gods.*
*My Beloved Brother Condemned,*

*I know you will understand because you understand this dwarf and brother condemned really well. As I before said to you, I am the free man who got the right to dispose of his self. This life is the only life, and it is a good life because it is the only one we have. I was born a small man with a big man inside, the flying-fox with an eagle in the gut. All my life I tried for to free this eagle so he can fly high and dazzle the world. Anyway, on this my last day and hour, you will find the eagle flying on the mango tree with his one wing of rope. Life, as I said and always wanted to preach to you, is good. It is good because it is ridiculous like a dwarf is ridiculous, an accident caused when parents make-fire too much. Because life is ridiculous it has to end the most ridiculous way, in suicide like Christ. Laugh, Pepesa, because I am right there inside the death-goddess which no one believes in anymore, and her sacred channel is all lava. Laugh, Pepesa, because her lava machine is grinding me, the Flying-Fox, to dust. Laugh, Pepesa, because there is nothing else to do.*

*The papalagi and his world has turned us, and people like your rich but unhappy father and all the modern Samoans, into cartoons of themselves, funny crying ridiculous shadows on the picture screen. Nevermind, we tried to be true to our selves. That is all I think any man with a club can do.*

*To you, your godly Excellency, I apologise because the Flying-Fox has nothing to leave in this my will, but 1001 laughs, as the movies say, which I desire you, your Excellency, to laugh one laugh every night from now on until you die. One laugh laughed loud will keep away sorrow and your father and the Romans and the L.M.S. and the modernaitu and the police and the Judge and bad breath. One laugh will turn everything to lava and joy and forgiveness.*

141

*For all this wealth I am leaving you, your most intelligent Excellency, I ask one last tiny favour. It is this – Dig a small hole on the bank of the Vaipe and into this hole dump this dwarf carcass of mine. Then fill it fast with Vaipe mud before it stinks our most excellent Vaipe neighbourhood. Plant on it taro and I swear on the lava that the taro will grow like nobody's business because I am excellent manure. When the taro is ready, give it to the market people. I am sure, as I am sure I am dead, that they will all die from greedy diarrhoea.*

*So long, Pepesa, I am moving down and out, as the cowboy says.*

*All is well in Lava. Tell your son and my nephew that, but do not tell Susana who, as your Excellency knows, is a bitch.*

> *I remain forever dead,*
> *Your humble self,*
> *Tagata, the Flying-Fox in the Mango.*

I bury him on the banks of the Vaipe.

# Exit

It is hot in my hospital room, so hot it is hard to breathe especially when I have rotten lungs. This morning the nurse tells me my father came again to try and see me; he comes every day but I refuse to see him. I look out the window, the two old men are stoking their fire as usual. The pain is getting too hard to bear. As usual the nurses are fixing the beds in the next ward. The old woman patient next door is dead, she died last night, her family collected her corpse this morning, there was much weeping and wailing. But hospital life goes on as usual.

I got out of bed this morning after the nurse bathed me and I carried my skeleton to the mirror. When I looked at the man in the glass I find him a stranger and an ugly one at that. The skin hangs off his bones like old clothes. The eyes have no laughter in the hollow sockets. The skull is rising to the surface of his face, soon the skull will have no skin-face. Only white bone. I staggered back to bed and coughed out the blood. I lay there as usual and waited for the doctor's visit.

They enter, the nurse and the red-haired doctor. I hide my pain and is the usual gay self. The doctor smiles and examines the patient on the bed. I watch his hands as they go over the body, the skin and bone, and pronounce it living still. He tells the nurse in English to give me the usual medicine. The nurse writes it down.

'Is it alive?' I ask him in English. He is surprised because it is the first time I have spoken English to him. I laugh and repeat the question.

'What is alive?' he asks.

'This body' I reply.

He laughs and says, 'Yes, it will rise and go home soon.'

'That is what you think,' I joke.

'You will be alright.' He does not laugh now. The nurse leaves.

'Have you make fire with her yet?' I ask. He does not know what I am referring to. 'With the nurse? She is mad on you.'

He stands up and his face is red like his hair. 'I am married,' he says.

'That does not matter,' I reply.

'My wife will not understand.'

'A pity. That nurse can teach you much,' I laugh. He is smiling this palagi who has become my first palagi friend.

I have forgotten my novel on the table near my bed. He sees it and says, 'What are you writing?'

'A letter.'

'A long letter, is it not? Who is it to?'

'To my self,' I say. There is an amazed stare on his face.

'It is in English?' he asks. I nod the head. 'Well, happy writing!' He walks to the door.

'I am going to die, am I not?' I call. He stops but does not turn to face me. 'Am I not? I want you to admit it to me.'

'Yes,' he says. He turned to look at me.

'Think of that nurse,' I tell him.

He leaves the room.

I continue to write this for the last time.

From the world of Sapepe, which my father destroyed by changing it, I came. From the world of Lupe and my aiga to the world of the Vaipe and Tagata and all my other friends, only to find them steps toward my self and my end. From the dark of Lupe's womb to the other dark of the death-goddess, I, Pepesa, has travelled and has seen what there is to be seen and felt and done what there is to do, and I found laughter.

Last night as I lay in my bed after the pain left me and sleep came, I dreamed I saw the lava field, black like sea, flow in to cover Sapepe, the Vaipe, Apia, the marketplace and all the mistakes and monuments we make to our selves. And I found my self above the lava sea as it flowed in deep and forever. And like the sun in the sky I saw Tagata laughing as he hanged from the freedom tree.

A few more sentences and I am done with this novel about my life. A few more and I am done. Outside the hospital window the baldheaded men are feeding their fire.

The maggots are impatient. Soon they will break out from my flesh like bubbles as beautiful as diamonds.

All is well in Lava, so spake the Flying-Fox.

# Virgin-wise —
# The Last Confession
# of Humble Man
# who is Man got Religion

Dear reader I had no school – no write no read no number no nothing. But I a man got big dream, got big everything. They tell me I no good for anything. But I a man still. I come from small village got church so I religion got. I come from home got big love so I got love for everybody. I come from land got holy music so I got music sing. I come got laugh from mother-womb so I got laugh for everybody. I come from land got hot woman so I women got in the oil. So tell reader if I no man or not? I got allthing you got. Got God too. So why not me a man? But that not what I go tell about. I go tell about this woman I got me, this woman I carry like second soul. Everybody got soul. But I got soulbusiness and I this woman got. You reader this woman got too. If you woman reader you man got like this my woman. This woman name Virgin-wise. She no face got one time, then she got face other time. Maybe face of your mother maybe face of your girlfriend maybe face of your granny maybe anyone face. She no got body then she body have like beauty queen or anybody you in your head got. She like God, is Virgin-wise. She allwhere – under bed over bed in bed – depend you tell her how behave. But she not like God who love everybody. She love nobody cause she nobody then she somebody, depend on you. You tell she love you. She love you. You make her do allthing real women no-do cause they virgin with strongchurchgoing, for Virgin-wise you make with no religion, make her evil-sin bad full of heat for to love you hot. Virgin-wise not only my woman mine. She all men woman. She girl in all men dream day or night or anytime. She like God faraway, every fellow part yet no part of every fellow. She like God cause you make her what she are. Like God you go cry to her. Like God you tell her your trouble your love your everything. And she no say boo. She your silent soul, you no-voice bedfire. You tell her talk she talk like you want her talk you. She like your child. You nurse she, you change she make she what you want. She same like Hine-nui-te-Po – hot fire dangerous like randy tiger. Till you want alltime with she, lie on she till you start fry and go scared and want fly away. But you no go fly away. She allwhere wait like death for you. Then you go make final choice. You want go 'holy-life-hereafter'. You like Maui want be cheeky to she. Then Hine-nui cross her leg boy, and you there-in no reach 'life with angel choir'. You flesh-bone mortal like me. I no thinker-man. But I a man. I know cause I been long-life with Virgin-wise. You no feel her you no see her you no hear her. But she there leech in your blood. And she grow on you like cross of wood grow to palm tree. But Virgin-wise she better than you wife, your part-time girl you feel see makefire with. She no tell you love her. She no howl and tell you you no good husband. She no nag you. She good girl behave. To dreamland she drive you boy cause she a dream. You tell her go to hell but she never say boo. You bedtime she, she no complain she go have night-time offspring. She no worry cause you no worry. Some people know I, say they no got Virgin-wise. They tell better thing they have, like idea. But this think-business and plenty-idea just shove in place of Virgin-wise. They makefire with plenty-idea they go mental bedtime with plenty-idea. This not real. This too dry too dead cause all in head. Not like me. I go got Virgin-wise see. She far real than plenty-idea. You do allthing with she and she still same. She virgin stay. She Virgin-wise.

Dear reader I no thinker-man. I just humble man remember good. I remember I got have first my Virgin-wise. Twelve year I was, just small fry with no big-stand. One night I sleep. I dream Virgin-wise came and I came bad. I was stood inside big cave dark and damp like belly of whale – Jonah deep in belly of whale – and someone soft put soft-soft hand on I, and whisper 'Boy, you got it!'

Reader I real had bad. I look and there was her – naked and ready-eating suckling pig. She was widow who live down road. She use go with many men. She use makefire with anyone come rain come sun. There she stand I no lie tell now. She naked as day she born. And she float to me and clutch I. Reader I real came first time. Quick I wake found sleep-sheet real wet. And I tell me I sin cause it no good boy who dream bad dream like that. It sin to come so preacher say on Sunday. It sin lust after woman-meat. And boy I shiver and shake for fear of holy God's wrath when I wake find sheet stiff and me feel like heaven all over. Next day I too ashame bad to look at widow cause she know and may yell 'Sinner-man there!' and point finger at me. But I tell me that I safe for she only in dream – black-secret dream which belong to me. God no punish me. And so I no worry anymore. I like dream happen again. But it never come for week. So I begin make bedfire to widow in sinful head before I drop sleep every night time. She never complain or tell me no. In school when bored I use sit and go dreamland with my Virgin-wise. Child-story you tell me but it too real be fairytale. At night widow turn to face-without-woman Virgin-wise and I sweat and me abuse me forget it sin to do. Most time I listen other boys tell about bedtiming women just like me makefire with Virgin-wise. One day me find under hedge with real-flesh then know I other boys tell lie. It not so hot for real. For she may not come and she scratch and swear at you. But Virgin-wise she never complain. She always satisfy. I no tell lie boy. Truth I have for religion I got.

Then when I twenty year me and Virgin-wise got marry young girl name Masina. She beautiful like nobody's business. She obey me always, always do like I tell her do. But she never talk with me and she too dead in bed. She not like Virgin-wise who do allthing with no blushing or shy. Then first child come and Masina become big-mouthed. She nag me alltime. But she no worry me cause I got Virgin-wise who far married to me than Masina. Masina have too many relative who stand with she against Virgin-wise and me. It go got too bad I knock Masina a few time. She leave me. Reader I no cruel husband. But Masina too bad for me. I no care much at time for I got Virgin-wise. Marriage is dead cell, reader. Too much worry and man no free from self.

After Masina run off I try other real-flesh but they still no good like Virgin-wise. Virgin-wise everywhere other women nowhere but in themself, too worry about themself and expect all men like 'Tuialamu with Big-Stand' or 'Prince on White Stallion'. They too selfish no grow up like Virgin-wise.

So reader I now grey, wrinkle like over-ripe mango and got no real-flesh worry me. I got Virgin-wise. She never leave me. She in my soul. And she grown on me like second head. But I safe. Don't care if she be Hine-nui-te-Po cause soon I in there die, die in she like Maui. But who care – all has to die. But I die sweet death and make smile deadman. You die too reader maybe with your Virgin-wise cause she in everybody. But if you reader are fellow who makefire with plenty-idea then you no die sweet death like me – cause plenty-idea too dry too dead for it all in head. Goodbye dear reader I go now meet Virgin-wise. She wait for me round corner in corner over corner – in I like Hine-nui-te-Po. Forgive dear reader please confession of humble man who is man got religion.

# Glossary

| | |
|---|---|
| afakasi | half-caste |
| aiga | family, extended family |
| aitu | ghost, evil spirit |
| faafafine | effeminate man, homosexual |
| faamafu | home-brewed beer |
| fale | Samoan house |
| fuia | bird, usually with black plumage |
| ietoga | fine mat |
| iofi | tongs made from the rib of coconut leaf, used for picking up the hot stones of a stone oven |
| lali | large wooden drum |
| lavalava | wrap-around, worn round waist |
| malae | meeting area |
| matai | titled head of an aiga |
| paepae | stone foundation of a fale |
| palagi, papalagi | person of European stock |
| puataunofo | large yellow flower |
| segasegamou | small bird |
| sene | Samoan cent |
| siva | to dance (v.), a Samoan dance (n.) |
| taamu | (giant taro), large edible bulbous root |
| talie | large tree found near the coast |
| tamaligi | tamarind tree |
| talo | edible bulbous root |
| tusitala | writer |
| umu | stone oven |
| valusaga | short stake pushed into ground, used to scrape food on |